D1108776

New Guinea
Moon

Also by Kate Constable

Crow Country
Cicada Summer
Always Mackenzie
Winter of Grace
Dear Swoosie (co-written with Penni Russon)

The Chanters of Tremaris series
The Singer of All Songs
The Waterless Sea
The Tenth Power
The Taste of Lightning

Kate Constable

New Guinea Moon

ALLEN&UNWIN
SYDNEY·MELBOURNE·AUCKLAND·LONDON

First published in 2013

Copyright © Kate Constable, 2013

Allen & Unwin
83 Alexander Street
Crows Nest NSW 2065
Australia
Phone: (61 2) 8425 0100
Fax: (61 2) 9906 2218
Email: info@allenandunwin.com
Web: www.allenandunwin.com

A Cataloguing-in-Publication entry is available from the
National Library of Australia
www.trove.nla.gov.au

ISBN 978 1 74331 503 3

Cover design by Kirby Stalgis
Cover photos by Lynn Koenig/Getty Images
Set in 11/16.5 pt Sabon by Midland Typesetters, Australia
Printed and bound in Australia by Griffin Press

10 9 8 7 6 5 4 3

MIX
Paper from
responsible sources
FSC® C009448

The paper in this book is FSC certified.
FSC promotes environmentally responsible,
socially beneficial and economically viable
management of the world's forests.

For my parents, with love and gratitude

1

December 1974

Julie stands in the doorway of the plane. The heat slaps her in the face like a hot, wet towel. Passengers crowd at her back, impatient to disembark. Sunlight blazes in her eyes as she picks her way down the steps to the tarmac. Instant sweat prickles on the back of her neck, itching under her ponytail. Brown-skinned local workers stand about, hands on hips, calling to each other in words she can't understand. Pidgin: that's what they speak here. She knows that much. Palm trees dangle their fronds, drooping and exhausted in the shimmering heat.

She's never been anywhere like this before. The air is so thick with humidity it's like trying to breathe soup. The sun presses down on the top of her head, as relentless as a hot iron.

Tony doesn't live in Port Moresby. She has to catch another plane to a different town, even smaller and more obscure, called Mt Hagen, a dot in the middle of the map.

The terminal building is hardly more than a glorified shed. Inside, the overhead fans turn languidly, barely disturbing the air. While Julie waits to have her passport checked, sweat dampens her forehead and rolls down inside her dress. Dark faces are all around, though the official who stamps her passport is white, and his voice is broad Australian.

'Have a nice holiday, love.' He gives her a wink.

Julie gathers up her papers without answering. For half a second, she contemplates telling the man, *In a few hours from now I'm going to meet my father for the first time since I was three.*

It had started almost as a joke, as a challenge to her mother during one of their endless arguments. She can't even remember now what Caroline said to spark it off, but Julie had snapped back, hot with fury, *Well, maybe I should go and live with Tony for a while and see how that works out!* And Caroline, suddenly calm, had said, *Maybe you should . . . Yes, maybe after thirteen years, it's time you two got to know each other.*

And the next thing she knew, it was all arranged, and Julie was heading to New Guinea for the summer holidays, while Caroline took a solo trip to Sydney, which hardly seemed fair. She'd never taken Julie to Sydney.

Julie doesn't tell all this to the man in the official uniform. Instead she says, 'I need to catch a flight to

Mt Hagen with Highland Air Charters. Could you please tell me where I have to go?'

Sweat trickling down her back, carrying the mustard-coloured vinyl suitcase and the brown overnight bag Caroline lent her, Julie struggles through the terminal. In front of her, blocking her way, two Australian men, wearing shorts and long socks, stroll with treacle-like slowness.

'Excuse me!' says Julie loudly. The men half-turn, as if surprised to see her there, but they don't move aside to let her pass. *If I was tall and blonde and gorgeous, they'd let me through.* She is not tall and blonde and gorgeous; she is ordinary, with mid-length mousy hair and freckles across her nose. Scowling, she dodges around the two men and almost trips over the outstretched legs of a local man who is slouched against the wall.

People are sitting on the ground, anywhere they can find a spot, in family groups, chatting and sharing food. A woman leans back, her eyes closed, while her baby suckles at her bare breast, his head tipped back, his bright brown eyes wide and searching, gazing around at the upside-down world.

Julie drops her luggage and rummages in her shoulder bag for a hanky to mop her sweaty face. She looks up and her bags have disappeared.

It takes her a second to realise what has happened. Then she sees a flash of mustard vinyl, weaving through the crowd up ahead. A man has taken her bags and trotted away with them.

'Hey!' shouts Julie. 'Hey, come back! Put those bags down! Thief! Thief!'

She starts to run. Her legs feel like lead, like legs in a nightmare, but anger fuels her, drives her onward. 'Stop!' she shouts. 'Hey, you, stop!'

People scatter before her, startled eyes turning on her. She's gaining on him; she can almost touch him. She gathers herself and leaps, hurling her weight onto his back, pummelling him with her fists. 'Stop, give me back my bags!'

He's not a big man, and he crumples beneath her. There's a soft *whuff* as his breath is knocked out of him. The brown bag and the suitcase go flying. Locked together, Julie and the thief crash to the floor of the terminal.

'Hey. *Hey*. What's all this?'

Julie sees a pair of brown shoes, and the inevitable long blue socks. A firm hand grips her shoulder and pulls her to her feet.

He's a young man. His skin is the colour of milky tea, though his accent is as Australian as Julie's own. She feels his hand burning through the fabric of her cotton dress onto her shoulder; the next instant, he lifts it away.

'This man is stealing my luggage!' she says, breathless.

The thief still cowers on the ground, as if he's scared she might attack him again. Julie smoothes her hair with her hand, a little embarrassed.

The young man speaks to the thief in rapid, stern Pidgin. The thief answers, scrambling to his feet.

The young man turns to Julie. 'He wasn't.'

'What?'

'He wasn't stealing your bags. He was helping you to carry them. He's a porter.'

'Bull!' says Julie hotly. 'He just took off with them. He didn't ask me; he didn't even know where I was going. If he's a porter, where's his uniform? Where's his badge?'

A suppressed smile creases the corners of the young man's eyes; then he makes his face stern again. Once more he speaks to the bag-snatcher. The bag-snatcher replies, wide-eyed with indignation. They argue back and forth for a minute or two. Julie is conscious of people staring at them. She manages to find her hanky at last and wipes her flushed face.

At last the young man turns to her. 'You do need a porter, don't you? Those bags look pretty heavy. Or is someone meeting you?'

'No . . . I'm catching another flight.'

'Then why not let this guy carry your bags for you?' says the young man reasonably.

'No way!' says Julie. 'I'm not letting a thief take my luggage. He's not even a successful thief,' she adds.

The thief looks at her with venom. Julie is sure he can understand what she's saying. She folds her arms and glares back at him. She says loudly, 'You're lucky I haven't called the police!'

The young man laughs. He reaches into his pocket and pulls out a handful of change. He counts out a couple of coins and the maybe-thief's hand closes eagerly over them, tight as a trap. '*Raus!*' says the young man. 'Go on, get lost.'

The man scurries away.

'What did you give him money for?' Julie says. 'If he is a porter, he didn't earn it, and if he's a thief, he doesn't deserve it.'

'If he's a porter, you've besmirched his reputation, and he should get some compensation. If he's a thief, as you pointed out, he's not a very good one. You've got to feel sorry for him, really.'

Julie opens her mouth, then closes it again. 'Well,' she says grumpily. 'Thanks. I guess.' She fishes in her shoulder bag for her purse.

'Hey, what are you doing?'

'Paying you back.'

'Forget about it.'

'But it's not fair; I can't let you —'

'I haven't got time,' says the young man. 'I've got a plane to catch —' he glances at his watch, '— ten minutes ago. I'd better run.'

'Oh, no!' cries Julie, stricken. 'That's my fault!' She throws the strap of the overnight bag over her shoulder, snatches up her own case and seizes a small suitcase from the young man's hand. 'I'll help with your luggage. Where are we going?'

'This way, but —'

Julie doesn't wait to hear his protests. She just runs, and the young man jogs easily beside her. He isn't sweating; he looks cool and slightly amused. Side by side they run through the terminal and onward to the domestic terminal.

'Where —?'

'This way — Talair.'

The young man draws up in front of the Talair check-in desk. Julie dumps the bags at her feet and pants for breath while he asks the afro-haired girl behind the counter, 'Flight to Mt Hagen?'

The girl shakes her head. 'You're too late, sir.' She waves her arm at the big glass door. 'It's just taking off now.'

Julie can see a black-and-white plane trundling down the runway. The young man slaps his hand flat onto the counter and swears beneath his breath.

'It's all right,' says Julie. She touches his arm. 'I don't know your name —'

'Simon,' says the young man wearily. 'Simon Murphy.'

'I'm Julie McGinty. And I think I can help. Did you say you were going to Mt Hagen?'

'I *was*,' says Simon.

'But that's perfect. You can come with me. I'll get you a seat on my flight. It's my father's airline,' she says grandly. 'Come on. I'll fix everything.'

Simon casts her a wary look. 'Are you sure?'

'Of course. It's my fault you missed your plane — well, sort of. It's the least I can do.'

'I mean, are you sure you can fix it?'

'Oh,' says Julie. 'Well, I can try.'

The waiting area for Highland Air Charters is not far away. It consists of a row of plastic chairs and a sign — a logo of a blue bird inside a white circle, with the company name curved in blue letters beneath. A young white man in a pilot's shirt, with epaulettes and wings, is sitting in one of the chairs, his legs outstretched. His golden head is tipped back, his eyes fixed on the ceiling as he whistles tunelessly between his teeth.

As Julie and Simon hurry towards him, he slowly

reverts to the vertical. 'Hello,' he says amiably. 'Don't tell me. You're my passenger. You must be Juliet.'

He smiles suddenly, and his strong, tanned hand shoots out to grip hers. He has a tally-ho, Royal Air Force moustache, exactly the kind of moustache you'd expect a pilot to have.

'It's just Julie,' she stammers. 'Not Juliet.'

His blue eyes crinkle when he smiles. 'But you are Tony McGinty's daughter? I am flying you to Hagen?'

'Yes . . .'

He gives a small ironic bow. 'I'm your captain for today, Andy Spargo.'

Reluctantly Julie lets go of his hand. He is extremely handsome. 'This is Simon. I know this is a bit cheeky, but — is there any room on the plane for one extra?' She glances around at the empty waiting room. 'There don't seem to be any other passengers.'

'No,' agrees Andy. 'This is kind of a special run. We have got cargo, though.' He gives Simon an appraising look.

'Simon's missed his flight, and it was my fault. He was helping me sort out — a misunderstanding. I promised I'd ask . . .' Her voice trails away. Suddenly it seems a ridiculous favour to ask, of a complete stranger; absurd, to try to trade on Tony working for HAC. A slow blush begins to creep up Julie's neck.

9

'Oh, I think we can squeeze him in,' says Andy cheerfully. 'How much do you weigh, mate? Seventy kilos? Seventy-five?'

'About eleven stone,' says Simon. 'Plus luggage.'

Andy lifts one of Simon's bags and then the other, with a calculating expression. 'Should be right,' he says. 'You wouldn't have more than twenty kilos there, I reckon.' He claps his hands together. 'Chop chop! Better jump in the *balus*, or we'll miss the gap.'

He takes a suitcase in each hand and swings through the glass doors and out onto the tarmac. Julie follows, with Simon behind her. Though it has been far from cool in the terminal, the heat outside breaks over her in an oven-blast and her knees wobble.

'Thank you,' says Simon quietly behind her.

'Well, thank you,' says Julie. 'I suppose.'

And for the first time, they smile at each other.

2

'You don't live in Hagen, do you?' Simon says, as they hurry across the baking tarmac after Andy.

'Just visiting,' says Julie. 'For the holidays. How did you know?'

Simon shrugs. 'I know most of the expats in Hagen. There aren't that many of them.' Seeing Julie's blank expression, he adds, 'Expats. Expatriates. Aussies. Americans.'

'You sound like an Aussie yourself.'

'My dad's Australian. Or used to be. I went to boarding school in Brisbane.'

'And you live in Mt Hagen?'

'My father owns a coffee plantation just outside town.'

'A plantation! Like in *Gone With the Wind*?'

'Not exactly,' says Simon dryly. 'No slaves.'

Julie feels her face grow hot. His dad was Australian, but what about his mother?

Andy halts beside a blue-and-white striped plane. Compared with the plane Julie had flown in to Port

Moresby, this one is so tiny it might have been a toy. Her dismay must show in her face, because Andy laughs and says, 'Don't fret, Juliet. This is a tough little crate. Beechcraft Barons, the best balus ever made for the Highlands. They can be twitchy little buggers, but you're in good hands with me. Nothing to worry about. Ever flown in a light plane before?'

'Never.'

Andy shakes his head. 'And to think you're Tony McGinty's daughter.' He climbs inside and begins rummaging about, rearranging the cargo. He pokes his tousled head out, grinning cheerfully. 'Heaps of room. Chuck up the bags, will you?'

'Everyone flies up here,' says Simon. 'We have to, because the roads are so bad, and the mountains are so rough.'

'You want to sit up front, with me?' says Andy. 'You can be my co-pilot.'

Julie is annoyed that they are both speaking to her as if she were a frightened child. 'I'll be fine in the back,' she says shortly.

Andy and Simon exchange a flicker of a glance, and she knows that this is what her mother calls *being difficult*. She doesn't care. She ignores Andy's proffered hand and climbs into the back of the plane.

She hears Andy say to Simon, 'We'd better get a move on. We're running a bit behind schedule.' He scans the horizon. Indigo clouds are massing above the mountains. 'Should be right,' he murmurs uneasily, then ducks away to the other side of the aircraft, apparently performing some kind of last-minute inspection.

Julie fumbles with her seatbelt. 'There's nothing wrong, is there?'

Simon, settling himself in across the narrow aisle, glances out of the window. 'I don't think so.' He looks back at Julie.

'You do this a lot?'

'Hundreds of times.'

The whole plane shakes as Andy steps onto the wing and into the cockpit. It feels as flimsy and crushable as a soft drink can. Julie's hands are sweating. She shoves them under her thighs to stop them trembling, and hopes Simon hasn't noticed. They haven't even taken off yet, and already she feels sick with dread.

Andy slams the door shut with a heavy metallic *thunk*. 'All belted up back there?' he calls, and without waiting for a reply, he lowers a pair of big padded headphones over his ears.

The engines roar into life, the propellers whip into an instant blur. A crackle of static issues from Andy's headphones, a stream of indistinct words that must be instructions from the control tower. Andy answers, his words drowned by the din of the engines, and the little plane begins to trundle down the runway. Julie's heart is banging in her chest.

Faster and faster, the Baron races along the bitumen. The whine of the engines intensifies, the plane shudders, and then Julie feels a lifting sensation in the pit of her stomach. They are airborne.

Andy swings the plane around, tilting it so they can see the whole of the airport spread below, and the small, hot, dusty city of Port Moresby, trapped between the ranges and the turquoise sea. Then he straightens out and heads for the mountains.

This feels completely different from flying in a large aeroplane. That is like being sealed inside a steel canister, there is hardly any sensation of movement. But now Julie can feel the buffet of the wind, the roller-coaster of the air currents. For the first time she understands that the air is a separate element, like water — not just an empty space, not an absence, but a real force. They are gliding through the sky and the sky is holding them up; they are suspended in the air the way a fish is suspended in the ocean. She could reach out of the window and trail her fingers through the clouds. They are pillars of frozen sea-froth, towering on either side of the little droning Baron.

Julie stares down, hypnotised by the swiftly moving landscape below the meringue-heaps of the clouds.

Flying over Australia, she'd been bored by the endless flat monotony of the continent. But New Guinea's mountains are violent, jagged, crumpled, chaotic. Unbroken jungle drapes across the ridges like lush fur. The clouds drift silently past, ink-stained with blue and grey and silver.

The white noise of the engines fills Julie's head. Suddenly she realises that she's not scared any more. She can't tear her eyes from the enchanted map that moves beneath them. Sometimes the tiny fleck of the plane's shadow flickers below, leaping the side of a mountain slope or diving into the darkness of a steep valley, like the shadow of a tiny fish swimming between the sun and the sand.

This is Tony's job. No wonder he'd come here, for the chance to do this every day —

Only an hour to go before she meets him.

And then, without warning, they plunge into whiteout. The Baron bucks and judders in the heart of a cloud; rain drives against the windows in a roaring curtain. Andy shouts something over his shoulder. Simon's lips move, but it's impossible to hear what he's saying.

Julie clutches her hands together. *Nothing to worry about; nothing to worry about.* The plane shakes as if in a giant's fist. It will stop soon. This can't go on. The plane will shake itself to pieces. Julie's stomach jolts into her throat, then plunges to the base of her spine.

Oh, God, don't let me be sick. The terror of vomiting grips her harder than the fear of dying.

It can't go on, but it does go on. It seems like hours before the Baron at last slides out of the clouds. The sudden descent makes Julie's stomach drop. Simon touches her shoulder, points through the window. 'That's Mt Hagen!' he calls.

Julie twists her neck to stare down. 'Is that it?' she yells. 'It's tiny!'

Simon shrugs. 'Ten thousand people,' he shouts. 'More or less.'

Julie stares down at the little buildings, the winding roads, laid out like a miniature village, with plasticine trees and model cars. And now the airport is below them, the grey slashes of the runways, arrow-straight across the chaos of green vegetation, and Andy is bringing them down, each drop in altitude echoed by a sickening plunge in Julie's gut. The tops of the trees rise toward them until they are level with the windows. There is a rough bump, then another, a skidding of brakes, and a long slow jolting ride along the tarmac to the far end of the airstrip, where they slew to a halt outside a low white brick building with a large shed — a hangar? A cargo shed? A warehouse? — attached to it.

Andy twists around to give her an apologetic smile. 'Sorry about the landing,' he calls over the dying whine of the engines. 'Just wanted to put her down before the rain sets in.'

Heavy raindrops are splattering the windshield.

'That's okay,' says Julie. 'Some people think it's fun, being scared out of your skin. They'd pay a lot of money for a thrill like that.' Her numb fingers fumble to unbuckle the seatbelt. Her insides are seesawing between terror and elation. Now the danger is over, adrenalin is racing through her veins and she feels drunk with the high of survival.

Andy stares out of the window. 'Uh-oh. Here's trouble.'

A short man is marching across the tarmac. He has a red face and a thatch of thick hair that must once have been fair but is now mostly faded grey. Even sealed inside the plane, even with the rain drumming harder and harder against the roof, Julie can hear him bellowing.

'What the fucking hell do you think you're doing, leaving it this late? What kind of a fucking idiot are you, Spargo?'

Julie says, 'Is that — that's not Tony, is it?'

Andy gives a shout of laughter. 'Nah, that's not Tony. That's the boss — Mr Crabtree to you. Well, here goes.' He grimaces ruefully at Julie, and clambers out into the rain. 'G'day, Curry!' he yells cheerfully. 'Got here as quick as I could. Julie was running a bit late —'

Mr Crabtree speaks over the top of him. 'I don't give a rat's arse how late she was bloody running! Do you know the rule? Well, do you? *Do you?*'

'No see, no go,' says Andy. 'But —'

'Look at this bloody rain!' roars Mr Crabtree. 'You could see through this, could you? What are you, bloody Superman?'

Andy stands meekly, head bowed, the rain trickling from his hair, while Mr Crabtree yells at him, the veins standing out like ropes on the side of his neck.

Simon is watching this scene through the window, his face impassive. Suddenly Julie remembers that she'd arranged for Simon to hitchhike on this flight; how is she going to explain that to this ranting madman?

Simon gives her a sideways look. 'Curry Crabtree — that's not your father?'

'No, no.' *Thank God*, she almost adds. 'That's my father's boss. I'll explain everything to him . . . I'm sure he'll understand.' Even to her own ears, she sounds unconvincing.

She looks out through the veils of rain. No one else is hurrying across the tarmac. But Tony must be here, waiting inside. In just a couple of minutes, she'll be meeting him.

She hitches her shoulder bag over her head, hastily reties her ponytail and wipes her shiny face on her sleeve. She knows she smells of sweat; she wishes she could brush her teeth, but there's nothing she can do about any of that. 'Wish me luck,' she says. Then she scrambles forward and climbs out of the plane.

3

She can't give herself time to think about it. She walks up to where Andy and Mr Crabtree are standing in the rain, and clears her throat. Andy sees her, but Mr Crabtree doesn't. It's not until Andy nods pointedly in her direction that Mr Crabtree wheels around. His eyebrows are beetled and his face is pink with rage.

'Yes? What?'

Julie thrusts out her hand. 'I'm Julie, Julie McGinty. My — Tony — I think he works for you?'

Mr Crabtree stares her slowly up and down. 'So you're Mac's little girl, are you?' He frowns. 'Not so little.'

'The thing is —' Julie swallows. Cool rain is trickling down the back of her neck. 'I asked this guy — he missed his flight, and it was my kind of fault, so I asked if there was room for him to come with us . . .'

'Eh? What?' Mr Crabtree spins around. Simon stands waiting beside the plane, one bag in each hand, calm and neat and respectable. Mr Crabtree stares sharply back at Julie. 'He's a friend of yours?'

'Well — I guess so. His name's Simon Murphy. I'm sure he can pay . . .' Julie falters, suddenly less certain of this than she had been.

'Murphy? Patrick Murphy's kid?' Mr Crabtree shouts toward the plane. 'Hey! You're Patrick Murphy's son, are you?'

Simon walks toward them, ignoring the rain. 'Yes, I am,' he says. 'And of course I'll pay for my ticket. I can pay for it now.'

He reaches into his pocket, but Mr Crabtree glares. 'To hell with that,' he says abruptly. 'This one's on the house.'

Simon gazes directly back at him. 'Thanks, but that's not necessary. I can afford it. And Murphys don't take charity.'

Mr Crabtree's face turns purple. 'Who said anything about bloody charity? Not me! Too proud to accept a gift, are you?'

Simon's face is expressionless. He opens his wallet and pulls out some notes. 'Will this be enough?'

Julie watches anxiously as the two men stare at each other for a moment. The rain spatters on the notes in Simon's hand. Simon's face is tense but calm; Mr Crabtree scowls fiercely.

At last Mr Crabtree snatches a single note from Simon's hand. 'That'll cover it.'

Simon gives a stiff nod. 'Okay. Thanks,' he says. 'Someone'll be waiting for me at Talair. I'd better go.' He turns on his heel and marches off through the rain, a bag in each hand.

Julie swallows. She knows she is not the kind of girl that boys like; she knows that he is probably too old for her, anyway. It's too much to expect that he might have left her his phone number, or asked for hers. But all the same, she thinks he could at least have said goodbye.

'Since you're making such a damn fuss about the rain,' says Andy, 'any chance we could get out of it?'

'You watch yourself, smart-arse,' growls Mr Crabtree, but he turns and stalks toward the terminal. Andy winks at Julie, and follows.

Two local men dressed in grubby T-shirts and ragged shorts are strolling barefoot across from the cargo shed. Julie knows that she looks like a drowned rat; it's almost a relief to know that she couldn't possibly look any worse. She crosses the tarmac and enters a cramped waiting area crowded with people: Andy, Mr Crabtree, a young woman with long flowing red hair, and half a dozen white men in pilot's uniforms. All the pilots turn to stare at Julie.

'What the hell are you doing over there?' bellows Mr Crabtree, and Julie braces herself. Is he about to start yelling at her now? But now Mr Crabtree is all affability. He drops his meaty hand on her shoulder and propels her across the floor. 'Julie McGinty! Come and meet your dad!'

A stocky, middle-aged man with a balding head peers out from around a doorframe.

'Jesus, Mac, get your arse out here! She won't bite.'

A wave of good-natured laughter runs around the waiting area. Tony is prised from his hiding place and pushed toward Julie.

'There you go,' roars Mr Crabtree triumphantly. 'Give her a kiss, for Christ's sake. It's not every day you meet your long-lost bloody daughter!'

Tony leans forward and gives her a rapid, clumsy peck on the cheek. The men cheer and laugh. Awkwardly father and daughter shake hands, hardly able to look at each other.

'Jesus, you're as bad as each other, you two,' says Mr Crabtree. 'You've got a chip off the old block here, Mac.'

'Lay off, Curry,' drawls Andy, lounging against the counter. 'They don't need a cast of thousands gawking at them.'

Julie throws him a grateful glance, and he winks at her swiftly.

Mr Crabtree squeezes her shoulder. 'Ah, go on, take her home. Dinner at our place tonight. Don't forget, or Barb'll tear me a new one.'

Tony picks up the vinyl suitcase and the brown overnight bag. 'Travelling light. That's the way.' He smiles shyly, and for the first time Julie notices the scar across his bald pink scalp, deep enough to lay her finger in.

'Go and clean yourself up, love,' says Mr Crabtree. 'Come and see us when you're feeling human. You must be buggered.'

Julie follows Tony out to the car park, where he throws her bags into a small white car. She climbs into the front seat and looks for a seatbelt, but there isn't one. She is finally here. Perhaps she has jet lag, but she feels as if she's walking through a dream.

Tony slips into the driver's seat.

'You'd be too young to have your licence?'

'I've got my learner's. Mum's given me a few lessons. She says every woman should know how to drive, how to cook, how to type and how to break a man's hand.'

Tony grimaces. 'Yeah, that sounds like Caroline.'

The airport is about ten minutes out of town. During the drive, Tony clears his throat, but he seems too nervous to speak, until he finally asks, 'How was your flight?'

'Good — fine, thanks.' Impulsively Julie adds, 'It's amazing, being in one of those little planes.'

'Yeah. Yeah, it's pretty good. New Guinea has the best flying in the world.'

Julie stares out of the car window. The downpour has passed, and the world is drenched in a vivid, rain-washed light. The luxuriant vegetation is a richer green than she has ever seen, the heavy clouds lined with silver and lead, the road a glistening black. They drive past a man, walking barefoot, his hands clasped behind him, a woolly cap on his head. A group of women carry string bags slung from their foreheads, resting heavy on their backs. Julie turns to stare, and one woman beams a wide smile. Julie gasps; her teeth seem to be stained with blood.

'That's just betel nut,' Tony says. 'They're all hooked on the stuff. Turns your teeth red. They spit it out all over the place. Watch where you walk, betel spit's everywhere.'

'What does it taste like?'

'I wouldn't know. I've never tried it. It's native stuff.'

'Oh.'

Julie turns her attention back to the window. They pass bushes laden with scarlet flowers, banana trees with fronds like ragged banners, a building painted bright, careless blue called Ah Wong Trading Co. Raindrops glitter on glossy leaves. Soon they begin to pass houses built for the tropics — fibro boxes with louvred windows, some mounted on stilts, some squatting close to the ground. Most of the windows are enclosed in cages of bars.

Tony turns the car into a muddy driveway. 'This is us.'

It's a semi-detached fibro unit, shabby and damp-stained, the paint peeling from the low porch at the front door. An angel's trumpet bush, weighed down with white lilies, spreads across the front window, and a hibiscus tree, splashed with pink crepe flowers, leans drunkenly beside the door. Poinsettias in scarlet and green, the colours of Christmas, line the gravel drive.

'It's pretty basic,' says Tony.

'The garden is gorgeous. It's *lush*.' She steps out of the car and sinks into ankle-deep grass.

'Yeah, everything grows pretty fast up here.'

He unlocks the front door and stands back to let her inside. 'I cleared out a room for you. It's a bit on the small side,' he says apologetically. 'Just through here.'

The front door opens directly into the living room, with a kitchen alcove tucked into the rear, near the back door. A shabby lounge suite, a scratched coffee table, a stereo cabinet with a record player and a large radio, and a dining table with three wobbly chairs crowd the living room. A large, startling, carved wooden shield hangs on one wall. Julie looks around carefully, but she can't see a television set.

Tony leads her to a tiny bedroom at the back of the unit, just large enough for a single bed, a bedside table, a chair and a small built-in wardrobe. The door of the

26

wardrobe hangs crookedly, as if someone has punched it. 'Had to scrounge around to find the furniture,' he says. 'Sorry it doesn't match.'

'I don't care if it matches.' Julie sits gingerly on the edge of the bed, which sags alarmingly. Tufts of chenille have been plucked from the orange bedspread, leaving bald patches. The floor is covered with greenish linoleum, peeling up at the corners. She says bravely, 'It's lovely. Really — comfortable.'

A Holly Hobbie poster has been taped to the wall beside the bed. Tony sees Julie's eyes rest on it.

'I guess I was expecting — more of a little girl, you know.' He shuffles awkwardly in the doorway. 'I didn't think. I can take it down.'

'No, don't do that. You can leave it there. I don't mind Holly Hobbie . . .' Her voice trails away. To avoid looking at Tony, she leans over to peer through the window behind the bed at the large untidy square of backyard. A cascade of intensely magenta bougain-villea pours over the fence, swarms over the water tank and twines through the metal cage around the window. Beyond the backyard, a valley slants away, then rises again, the far slope dotted with fibro houses, dense trees, rectangular garden plots and huts woven from cane and thatched with grass. 'Oh, wow! Do people really live there? In those grass huts?'

Tony leans down to see what she's staring at. 'Yep. Just like *National Geographic*. Well, I'll leave you to it. Bathroom's next door. S'pose you'd like to — unpack. Settle in. Just sing out if there's anything you need.' He backs out of the room.

'Um, I might need a towel.'

Tony shakes his head. 'Knew I'd bloody forget something. Barb Crabtree wanted to come over but I said I could manage.'

'Barb Crabtree?'

'Curry's missus. Curry Crabtree — Allan — you met him just now. The boss. We're going round there for dinner tonight. They've got a couple of kids your age, home from school for the holidays. We thought you could hang out together . . . when I'm at work, you know. They'll be company for you.'

'Okay,' says Julie, without enthusiasm. If only Simon Murphy had shown some interest; she could have spent the holidays sipping long drinks on the plantation verandah . . . Hanging out with a couple of unknown kids doesn't hold the same appeal.

While Tony rummages in a cupboard for a towel, Julie slumps on the bed, suddenly too tired to move. The red poinsettias, the purple of the bougainvillea, the dark glossy green of the banana trees and the garden plots spin and tumble in her head like bright shards inside a kaleidoscope. An idea struggles to form itself — something about the shabby unit with the bars on the windows, and the exuberant wildness outside; something about the sealed bubble of the little plane as it passed above the seething clouds and the impenetrable mountains; something about a tiny frontier town, surrounded by terrain so fierce that roads can't push through. Something about safe places, and fragile walls, and the wildness and the danger, the unknown, on the other side of the glass.

But she's too tired to puzzle it out now. She'd promised to ring her mum, to tell her she's arrived safely. But first she picks up the threadbare towel that Tony's found for her and goes to take a shower.

'What about the time —' Allan Crabtree wipes his mouth. 'What about the time you put your Islander down in such a hurry, brakes squealing, and you jumped out like your arse was on fire. You couldn't get out of that plane quick enough —'

Tony chuckles. 'And Curry here comes belting across the tarmac, screaming at the top of his lungs. *You're sacked! How dare you leave the effing plane in that state!*' He gives Julie a shy glance. 'Except he didn't say effing.'

'You were shaking like a bloody leaf,' says Allan. 'Shrieking like a girl. *There's a snake in the cockpit; there's a snake in the cockpit!*'

All the faces around the table, Tony and the four Crabtrees, turn expectantly toward Julie, for whose benefit these stories are being told.

'Oh, wow,' she says. 'A *snake*?'

Tony looks gratified. 'I was flying in some green tree pythons for Baiyer River —'

'That's a wildlife sanctuary,' says Ryan Crabtree, startling Julie with the first words he's spoken all evening. He is Allan and Barbara Crabtree's son, a year older than Julie, back from boarding school for Christmas. He shoots her a glance from under his long, slightly greasy hair. Julie had dismissed him earlier as sullen and miserable, but perhaps he is just shy. She supposes it isn't his fault that his dark, heavy eyebrows give him a perpetual scowl.

Barbara says, 'Tony, maybe you could take Julie out to Baiyer River while she's here.'

Nadine, the Crabtrees' thirteen-year-old daughter, chimes in quickly. '*I* want to go to Baiyer River. I've *always* wanted to go to Baiyer River. I want to see the baby deer —'

'Shut up, Nads,' mutters Ryan.

'Nadine,' says Barbara, 'Uncle Tony's trying to tell a story.' She pushes back her chair and lights up a cigarette; she had waved away a bowl of fruit and ice cream when the housekeeper brought around dessert. She lowers her eyelids, heavy with eye shadow. Barbara has a dark bob, stiff as Cleopatra's wig. She looks bored, as if she's heard all these stories a hundred times, but she commands, 'Go on, Mac.'

'Well,' says Tony. 'One of the buggers got loose in the cabin. I managed to pin it down with a box before we landed, but its tail was thrashing around like a bloody whip. But Curry was screaming and yelling blue murder, how he didn't give a f— didn't give a fig about any effing snake — Pardon my French, kids. Sorry, Barb . . . *You've got a responsibility to the flaming aircraft, get back in there and shut her down properly!'*

'I made him do it, too,' says Allan with satisfaction. 'Snake or no bloody snake.'

'Damn thing tangled itself up behind the instrument panel. Took us hours to pull the bugger out.'

Allan takes a swig from his stubby of South Pacific lager. 'Remember the day Peter Manser clipped a tree, going from Goroka to Lae? He landed at Lae and the old balus was knocked about a bit, leaves hanging out of the flaps and what-have-you. Someone said, what happened? Peter says, "Oh, I hit a bird." They said, "It must have been a bloody big bird." "Yes . . ." says Peter.'

'*It was sitting in a tree!*' chorus Ryan and Nadine.

Julie laughs. Barbara blows out a stream of smoke and smiles a faint, tight smile.

'Peter used to scare the —' Tony coughs, glancing at Julie and Nadine, '— scare the suitcase out of his passengers. He'd pretend to read a novel while he was flying along, turn the pages, cool as a cucumber. Scared 'em witless! All play-acting, of course.'

'Used to take out his false teeth and leave them lying around,' muses Allan. 'I found them, once, sitting on top of a bar in Madang.'

'You can laugh,' says Barbara sharply. 'But it's that kind of stupid behaviour that gets people killed.'

'What, leaving your teeth out?' growls Allan.

'Showing off,' says Barbara coldly.

'Just a bit of fun, Barb,' says Tony. 'No harm in it.'

Barbara flicks her cigarette over a yellow glass ashtray. 'The younger pilots see this kind of adolescent nonsense from men old enough to know better, and they think they have to compete, to show how macho they are. Look at Andy Spargo today, racing the weather. Look at Kevin Griffen.'

Tony and Allan fall silent. The only sound is the faint clatter of dishes from the kitchen, where the house-keeper has started washing up.

Nadine asks in a small voice, 'What did happen to Kevin Griffen?'

'He was killed,' says Allan shortly.

'Nineteenth of July,' murmurs Tony.

'I knew Kevin Griffen,' says Nadine, in the same thin, small voice. 'He was that tall guy, wasn't he? With the big mouth, like Mick Jagger?'

Ryan stirs. 'We all know who he was, Nads.'

'But what *happened*?'

There is a painful silence. At last Tony says, 'He was flying into Telefomin. He just disappeared. You know how rough the country is up there — never found any trace of him. Weather was shocking. He should have turned back, but he must have decided to go for it.'

'The clouds up here have rocks inside,' says Tony to the tabletop. 'That's what they say.'

Ryan meets Julie's eyes. 'They call them chocolate-box clouds, up here,' he says. 'You never know which ones have got hard centres.'

Julie looks away.

'Ex-MOA,' growls Allan. 'Always knew it was a mistake to hire him.'

'Mission of the Air,' murmurs Tony, seeing Julie's puzzled face.

'Those MOA bastards think they can get away with anything! Always flying into gaps that aren't there, because God Almighty's watching over them! Stupid pricks.'

'They do a lot of good work,' says Barbara. 'You've got some missionaries living next door, Julie. Graeme and Robyn Johansson. Remind me to give you a bundle of clothes to pass on to them, before you go.'

Ryan says, 'Which plane was it?'

'Hotel Alpha Kilo,' says Tony. 'One of the Barons.'

'The Barons can be twitchy little buggers,' says Julie.

Everyone looks at her, startled, and there is a gust of laughter.

'You want to keep an eye on this one, Mac,' says Allan. 'Jeez, she's quick! She'll be after your job before you know it.'

Julie can feel Ryan staring at her from under his heavy dark brows, but when she looks back at him, he drops his eyes.

The housekeeper, an elderly local woman with hair as grey as steel wool, emerges from the kitchen and pads around the table, collecting the empty ice cream bowls. The soles of her bare feet look as tough and pliable as rubber thongs. Julie gives her an embarrassed smile and hands up her bowl. The woman flashes a brief smile back. No one else around the table speaks to her or pays her any attention; she might be invisible. Julie has never been waited on by a servant before; she doesn't know the rules. Does the housekeeper live here? Does she have her own little house somewhere? Or does she live in one of those grass huts?

The others are discussing someone who has moved back to Australia.

Barbara says, 'You can't blame him; he's got no future here.' She gives a bitter laugh. 'Let's face it, none of us do.'

Julie leans forward. 'What do you mean?'

'She's talking about Independence coming next year,' says Ryan, slouching in his chair. 'You must have heard about it, it's been all over the papers for months.'

'New flag, new money,' says Tony. 'That's all it is.'

'More than that,' says Allan. 'Goodbye Aussie. They'll be running their own show.'

'They're running it now,' says Tony. 'They started self-government last year.'

'Still had the Europeans to hold their hands, though.'

'Europeans?' says Julie. 'Isn't it mostly Australians?'

Tony flaps a hand. 'All the expats get called Europeans. Doesn't mean they're from Europe. Though we have got Germans, Canadians, Dutch, all sorts . . .'

'It means white people,' Nadine explains, in a loud clear voice. A ripple of embarrassment runs around the table.

Barbara frowns. 'Nadine —'

'What? *What?* It *does*!'

Ryan says, 'So are we going to become PNG citizens?'

'May as well,' says Allan, and 'Certainly not!' says Barbara emphatically. They glare at each other.

'Haven't even set foot in Oz for fifteen years,' growls Allan. 'What's the point of hanging onto bloody citizenship? Our whole life's here. May as well sign up for it properly.'

'*You* haven't been down south for fifteen years,' says Barbara. 'I have. And what about the kids? They'll be at uni soon, getting jobs. Their future's in Australia, not here. If the New Guineans don't want us, we should just get out and leave them to it. See how they manage without us.'

Allan scowls. 'You've got to face facts, Barb. This place is our bread and butter. When Independence comes, they want us to make a choice, that's fair enough.'

Barbara ashes her cigarette. 'Any fool can see they're not ready to govern themselves. There hasn't been time to train the nationals up properly. Maybe in another twenty years . . . Why the rush, all of a sudden?'

'Bloody Gough bloody Whitlam,' says Allan. 'Don't get me started.'

Julie sits bolt upright. Her mother voted for Whitlam. They had a party at their house the night Labor won the election, beating the Liberals for the first time in twenty-three years. She says, 'Independence is a good thing, though. Isn't it? Nations should be run by their own people. You can't have empires any more.'

'Australia's hardly got an empire,' says Tony with a smile. 'It's just one country to look after!'

'A good parent takes care of the children until they're capable of looking after themselves,' says Barbara. 'Don't you think? That's just common sense.'

'I haven't seen my father since I was three, and my mother's sent me to New Guinea by myself,' says Julie. 'Maybe I'm not the best person to ask.'

Ryan gives a snort of suppressed laughter. It seems to explode into the uncomfortable silence which follows.

'Sorry, Tony,' says Julie. 'I didn't mean — I was just making a point.'

Tony gives an awkward smile and shrugs one shoulder. 'Guess I earned that one.'

'Serves us right for talking politics,' says Barbara abruptly. 'Cheese?'

She pushes the platter down the long table. Julie keeps her head lowered as she busies herself cutting a wedge of cheddar.

Tony clears his throat. 'I've got another story for you,' he says. 'Once upon a time, so they say, Curry here went off to visit the Controller of Civil Aviation. He didn't have an appointment, so they wouldn't let him in. Well, he marches up and down the office, effing and blinding — you know the way he does — and he insists that he has to see the Controller urgently, immediately! Secretaries start to cry, they threaten to call the police, but he won't go away; he won't give up. At last they let him in. And Curry throws a map down on the Controller's desk and stabs his finger down on it, and he yells, *this mountain is in the wrong bloody place! What are you clowns going to do about it?'*

Julie feels herself beginning to smile. 'What did the Controller do?'

Tony smiles back, enjoying himself. 'The poor bastard didn't even think about changing the map. Oh, no. He picked up the phone and ordered some bulldozers. *Come on, boys, we've got to shift that mountain!'*

Julie laughs, as Ryan groans and Nadine says, 'I've heard that story a million times.'

'Haven't we all?' Barbara scrapes back her chair and gestures to the lounge area at the other end of the long room. 'Shall we?'

The Crabtrees' house is large and white and built of brick, with an expansive, parquet-floored living and dining room opening out onto a big verandah and the valley beyond. It's a house built for parties. 'The most expensive house in Hagen,' Allan had told Julie with gruff pride before dinner. 'Every bloody brick flown in. Cost a fortune.'

Tony and Allan settle themselves in deep armchairs with tumblers of whisky and begin to talk shop — flight routes and business prospects, which plane is due for a service, which pilot has leave coming up. Barbara drops onto the couch, her eyes hooded as she lights up a fresh cigarette and leafs through a magazine. Julie hesitates for a second, not sure if she wants to sit next to Barbara, then sits down on the rug. Nadine plumps down beside her. Ryan slouches over to squat next to the stereo.

Without looking up, Barbara says, 'Put on something decent, for God's sake, not that horrible wailing you insist on subjecting us to.'

Ryan scowls, but he says nothing as he flicks through the LPs. Perhaps he hasn't heard.

'Has your housekeeper worked for you for a long time?' Julie asks Nadine.

'You mean Koki? Oh, yeah, she's been with us forever. She came when Ryan was a baby. She looked after both of us. She's kind of like another mother.' Nadine giggles. 'She's probably taken care of us more than Mum has.'

'I hardly think that's true,' says Barbara sharply.

Nadine pulls a face at Julie. 'It is, though,' she whispers cheerfully.

'What does she do when you and Ryan are at boarding school?'

'Who, Mum? I dunno!'

'I meant Koki . . .'

'Oh, she cleans and cooks and everything,' says Nadine vaguely. 'That's what *meris* do. Everyone here has a *meri* or a *haus boi* . . . And she looks after the animals, of course. There's Roxy the dog, and the birds, and George my cuscus . . . He's sort of like a possum.

He got his foot caught in a trap but I rescued him. Do you want to see him?'

'Okay,' says Julie, but she doesn't get up. She looks around the living room. 'Don't you have a TV either?'

Nadine laughs. 'There is no TV up here.'

'No television at all?' Julie stares at her.

'We make our own fun,' says Barbara briskly. 'Canasta nights, parties, the Drama Club. We have a terrific time, don't we, Ryan?'

'Yeah,' says Ryan. He lowers the needle onto a record and suddenly a Neil Diamond song blares into the room.

'Turn that down!' barks Allan. 'A man can't hear himself think with that bloody racket.'

Ryan flops into a chair.

'Why don't you kids have a dance?' says Barbara. 'Go on, Ryan, ask Julie for a dance.'

'Oh, no, I don't —' says Julie.

'God, Mum!' protests Ryan at the same moment.

They look at each other. Julie isn't sure whether to be grateful or offended that he seems as reluctant to dance with her as she is to dance with him.

'I'll dance,' says Nadine. She scrambles up and throws herself into an energetic shimmy.

'Show-off,' mutters Ryan.

'She does jazz ballet,' says Barbara. 'Do you do jazz ballet, Julie?'

'No. No, I don't. My mother —' She stops herself. She can't say, *my mother thinks jazz ballet is stupid.*

Barbara says sympathetically, 'Your mother will miss you while you're away.'

'I doubt it,' says Julie. 'When I rang her this afternoon she was all excited about going to Sydney to visit her friend.'

'Oh, well, she'll need to keep herself busy,' says Barbara vaguely.

That's never a problem, thinks Julie, but she doesn't say it aloud.

Carefully Tony sets his whisky on the table, then heaves himself out of his chair. 'Dance with an old man —?' He glances sideways at Julie, then loses his nerve. '— Barbara?'

'Why not?' She closes her magazine and stands up, smoothing her dress over her thighs, and she and Tony step out into the middle of the floor.

Ryan covers his eyes with his hand. 'It's kinder not to watch,' he mutters, and Julie can't help a giggle. In fact, she thinks, Barbara and Tony don't dance too badly, for old people. She vaguely remembers her mother saying something about Tony being a good dancer. Back in the days when Caroline believed in dancing . . .

Allan sits with his hands resting on the arms of his chair, like a medieval king on his throne, surveying his court. 'Mac!' he commands. 'Ask your daughter to dance with you, for Christ's sake. And get your hands off my wife!'

'What do you care?' says Barbara tartly. 'I could grow old and die waiting for *you* to ask me.' But she pats her hair and sits down.

Slowly Julie climbs to her feet. Tony is waiting, his arms hanging by his sides. She walks across the polished floor, feeling them all watching, certain that they're all exchanging secret smiles. Her face feels hot. Tony pulls a small private grimace, to show her he feels awkward too. Julie holds out her hands and Tony takes them, and they shuffle on the spot together. Julie fixes her eyes on the Christmas tree behind Tony's shoulder; Tony looks at the floor.

Then a new song comes on: 'Sweet Caroline'.

Instantly Tony and Julie drop their hands. Their eyes meet and they both begin to laugh. Tony shakes his head. 'Nah, mate, no — not that one.'

'What's so funny?' demands Nadine.

'Julie's mother is called Caroline,' says Barbara.

Julie says, 'She's not exactly sweet, though.'

'*I feel inclined* . . .' hums Ryan. He's watching Julie.

'Take the poor kid home, Mac,' Allan barks. 'She's dead tired. Look at her; she can hardly stand up.'

'I thought we'd take you to see the market tomorrow,' says Barbara briskly. 'We'll pick you up at nine.'

*

43

Exhausted as she is, Julie finds it hard to fall asleep. Her brain whirls with the people she's met and the things she's seen since this long day began. It seems years ago since she last went to bed, far away in a Brisbane hotel. Julie smiles to think how excited she'd been about staying in that hotel alone; it seems like another planet.

Frogs throb outside the window, pumping their calls out into the night. Julie gazes out into the darkness. A half-moon, like a tiny tin boat, sails in the sky high above. She lies down and closes her eyes. The frogs' song drums in time with her own heartbeat, steady, unhurried, a soothing beat . . .

Suddenly she is jolted from sleep. The moon has slipped down the sky, and a deep rumbling, like thunder, has replaced the frogs' chorus. Her bed is rocking gently to and fro. The window louvres chatter above her head. She puts her hand to the flimsy wall and it shivers beneath her palm. She must have let out a startled noise, because there are footsteps outside her door, and Tony's gruff voice calls out, 'It's all right, nothing to worry about. It's just a *guria*, an earth tremor. Happens all the time.'

'Okay — I'm okay,' she calls.

She lies down again as the tremor subsides, and feels her bed shaking, trembling, then gradually falling still. The distant grumbles fade away. On top of everything else, now an earthquake! She'll have to tell Caroline about that when she writes her first letter; though her mother won't believe it. Julie is still smiling into the darkness when sleep mows her down.

5

When she wakes, it takes her a second or two to remember where she is. Then anticipation fizzes through her and she shoots out of bed. She can hear Tony moving about in the bathroom; it was his alarm that woke her. It's barely light; a glance out of the window shows her a misty, chilly morning. She shivers into her clothes and out into the kitchen.

'You don't need to get up, Julie. Have a lie-in. I'll be off to work in a minute.'

'That's okay. I'm awake now.'

'Coffee?'

'Yes, please.' She opens the fridge. 'Is this long-life milk all there is?'

'That's it. Just UHT,' says Tony apologetically. 'There's no fresh — no dairy in Hagen. Not enough *bulmakaus*. Cows,' he adds.

'Yeah, I guessed.' She adds a splash of the milk to the mug that Tony offers her and takes a cautious sip.

'You get used to the taste,' says Tony.

'Really?' says Julie.

Tony grins. There's a tap at the door and he unlocks it. A tall thin man with sunken cheeks and a drooping moustache inserts one long leg through the doorway, like a stork. Julie recognises him as one of the pilots she saw at HAC yesterday.

'Gibbo lives in the unit next door,' says Tony. 'You'll probably hear him snoring through the wall. You after a lift, mate?'

'Thanks, mate.' Gibbo peers at Julie. 'Everything has beauty,' he says. 'But not everyone sees it.'

'What?' says Julie.

'Confucius,' says Gibbo.

Tony rolls his eyes. 'Gibbo thinks he's a philosopher. Just ignore him. Well, I guess I'll see you later.'

'Bye,' says Julie.

There is an awkward moment while they both decide that they don't know each other well enough yet to kiss goodbye. Julie lifts her hand, and Tony nods. 'Spare key is on the bench,' he says. 'Don't forget to lock up when you go.'

'Okay. See you. Nice to meet you, Gibbo.'

Gibbo's voice floats in from the front steps. 'He who chooses a job he loves will never work a day in his life . . .'

'You're full of it, mate, you know that, don't you?' says Tony, closing the door behind them.

Julie toasts some bread under the griller, washes up the few dishes, straightens her bed and tidies up the unit. She wonders why Tony doesn't seem to have a meri, if Nadine says that 'everyone does'. Then she makes another cup of instant coffee, and carries her mug outside into the fresh clean air of the garden. The mist has cleared and the sky is pale, scattered with puffy clouds. The grass is soft underfoot. The glossy leaves of the bushes gleam in the weak sunshine. The two units share the backyard; Julie wanders across into Gibbo's half of the garden, where she can see a well-tended vegetable plot. What is he growing? Carrots? The lush leaves look familiar, but she can't quite recognise them ... All at once she realises they're marijuana plants.

'Good morning!'

Julie starts back guiltily. A middle-aged woman is waving and smiling at her across the fence on the other side of the garden.

'You must be Tony's little girl!'

'Yes, I'm Julie.'

'Hi there! I'm Robyn.' Robyn has an American accent.

As Julie walks over to the fence she can see that Robyn wears a gold cross on a slim chain, and her hair is cut short in the unflattering style that she always associates, perhaps unfairly, with Christians.

'So we're neighbours now!' Robyn sings out cheerfully. 'Would you like to come visit a while? I have cookies.'

'Um . . .' says Julie. Caroline has brought her up to be suspicious of any organised religion. But it's only a biscuit; a biscuit can't do any harm, if she's on her guard. Hesitantly she says, 'Okay . . .' But then she remembers. 'I don't think I've got time, actually, someone's picking me up at nine o'clock.'

Even as she speaks, she hears a car pull up at the front of the unit, followed a moment later by hammering at the door.

'Next time!' cried Robyn, flashing a toothy smile. As Julie runs back inside, she is still smiling and waving over the fence.

Nadine is hopping from foot to foot at the front door. 'Ready?'

Barbara leans from the car window. 'Make sure you lock up properly!' she calls. 'Bolt all the doors, and don't leave any windows open! You have to be so careful here.'

Julie runs back and checks all the windows and doors, then runs out to jump in the car. Ryan is in front beside his mother, and Nadine's in the back.

'You haven't left any washing on the line, have you?' says Barbara, as she reverses swiftly out onto the road. 'Because they'll steal from the clothesline, too.'

'Once, we were driving back from the shops,' says Nadine, 'and there was a meri walking down the street wrapped up in one of our sheets!'

'Striped flannelette,' says Ryan gloomily. 'It was my favourite sheet.'

'I haven't washed anything yet,' says Julie. 'So our sheets are safe. For now.'

*

The market is a revelation. It's a crazy, chaotic festival. Barbara marches up to the gate, where a row of snot-nosed, barefoot urchins are perched on a fence, gnawing sticks of sugarcane. As they approach, the little boys spill off the fence and jostle around them, grinning and wriggling. *'Mi, misis, mi!'* Barbara gives one boy a copper coin and hands him her wide, flat-bottomed basket.

Julie feels a twinge of unease, watching him struggle with the outsized basket as it whacks against his scabbed, bony shins. Ryan could carry it easily. But then the boy would have missed out on the coin.

'Watch out for betel spit,' says Ryan over his shoulder.

'Ryan doesn't usually come to the market,' Nadine tells Julie. 'We're so-o-o honoured.'

'I had a craving for salty plums,' says Ryan loftily. 'For your information.'

'What are salty plums?' says Julie.

There's so much to look at. Small heaps of vegetables are piled on colourful cloths or woven mats, spread on the stony ground, or arranged on benches. Half-naked women preside over the stalls, giggling behind their hands as they gossip together. Julie sees one woman casually nursing a baby, her flat, stretched breasts flopping against her chest like a pair of brown socks. *Just like National Geographic*, she thinks, and she looks away, embarrassed.

There are pyramids of purple taro roots; hands of green and yellow bananas; knobbly sweet potatoes; glowing tomatoes; pineapples; bunches of peanuts tied by the stems, straight from the ground, dirt still clinging to their shells; long, lacquered sticks of sugarcane; plump pea pods; delicate baby carrots with their froth of foliage; severed heads of lettuce and cauliflower and broccoli; lemons, passionfruit, sweet corn, swollen yellow cucumbers.

An old woman with toothless gums and a face like a map of wrinkles sits behind sheaves of tobacco leaves. There are wooden carvings, necklaces of shells and strings of tiny coloured beads, folded piles of loose, brightly patterned tops. Julie shakes one out and holds it against herself.

'That's a meri blouse,' says Nadine.

'Oh!' Julie lays it down.

'But they're not just for meris. Everyone wears them, Europeans as well. You can buy one if you want to.'

'Of course I could,' says Julie hastily. 'But it — it wasn't really my colour.'

Somewhere in the distance, piglets are squealing in distress. Scrawny chickens flap in cages of split bamboo; puppies squirm and pant. The scent of wood smoke mingles with a musty odour. Julie wrinkles her nose and recoils a little as she realises that it's the smell of unwashed human bodies. For a minute she feels almost faint as two men strut past in traditional dress, resplendent in wide belts with rear skirts of bunched leaves, like bustles, over their naked buttocks.

Ryan follows Julie's gaze. 'You know what they call that? *Arse-gras*.'

'No,' says Julie. 'Really?'

'A beard? *Mausgras* — mouth grass. Hair? *Gras bilong het* — head grass.'

'You're making this up.'

Ryan shrugs. 'Cross my heart . . . I used to speak fluent Pidgin when I was a kid. But I've forgotten most of it now.'

Julie can't take her eyes off the villagers. Short and sturdy, they stride through the marketplace, feathers swaying in their hair. The moons of seashells from the far-off ocean glow pale against their dark chests. One man has thrust a cigarette casually through his pierced nose, and another has tucked a plastic lighter into his headdress, among strings of grass-seeds and slender cassowary feathers.

Ryan offers Julie his bag of salty plums, and cautiously she takes a small, hard, pinky-orange nugget. She says, 'It looks like a poo from a Technicolour rabbit.' She grimaces at the peculiar sour-sweet-salty tang, and Nadine laughs.

'Urgh!' Julie shudders. Then: 'Can I have another one?'

Sometimes Barbara stops to greet someone, or to wave and smile at an acquaintance. These friends are mostly women, and all of them are white. There are locals all around, but the Crabtrees don't seem to know any of them. Julie keeps a lookout for Simon Murphy, but she doesn't see him.

Slowly Barbara's basket fills with fruit and vegetables. Using the money her mother gave her, Julie buys a string bag. 'That's a *bilum*,' says Nadine. 'You'll have to wear it hanging off your forehead like a native.'

Julie shoots her an uneasy look. She is pretty sure that *native* is a word her mother would disapprove of. But maybe the rules are different here. And what should she say instead? Papua New Guinean? Indigenous person?

Ryan catches the look. 'We don't say *native* any more, Nads, remember? It's *national*.'

'Oh,' says Nadine. 'I forgot. Anyway, it's not as rude as *kanaka*.' She darts away to her mother's side and begins to beg for a puppy.

Well, that answers that question. 'I was just wondering what the right word was,' says Julie. '*Native* sounds so . . . colonial.'

'Yeah, well,' says Ryan. 'This was a colony.' He squints at her. 'A word to the wise? Just be a bit careful what you say. I mean, *we* know you're not a snob or anything, but you don't want people to get the wrong idea.'

'What's it got to do with being a snob?' says Julie. 'It's about —' She stops herself. She remembers how much she hates it when Caroline lectures her on Women's Liberation or civil rights. She says, 'I'm going to buy some fruit to put in my bilum.'

She buys a pineapple, some passionfruit, bananas and tomatoes, a bag of salty plums and a stick of sugarcane, just to see what it's like. Nadine shows her how to strip off the tough outer casing with her teeth, then chew on the fibres to release the thick, sweet, sticky juice.

Barbara sniffs. 'That will be the first fruit ever to cross Tony McGinty's doorstep.'

Julie doesn't even try to imitate Barbara's imperious haggling; she pays whatever the women ask. 'They expect you to haggle, you know,' Barbara warns her. 'They'll take you for a fool.'

'I don't mind,' says Julie. 'It's all so cheap, anyway.'

'The market is cheap. But the shops are so expensive . . .'

Julie closes her ears to Barbara's complaints. Drinking in the smells and colours, the rise and fall of voices, like a song whose words she can't quite catch, with the cool clear sunshine falling on her bare arms, she feels as if she's been asleep and is now waking up, blood tingling through her veins. But the sensation of coming to life is painful, too. The snotty, grubby children with their distended bellies, the dirt and poverty, the puppies with their rheumy eyes, the terrified shrieking of the pigs — the Crabtrees seem not to notice these things. Julie can't believe that a place so intensely beautiful can be simultaneously so distressing.

'There's Teddie Spargo!' exclaims Barbara. 'Teddie! Teddie! Over here!'

Julie sees the young woman with the long red hair who was in the HAC office the day before. She turns in her flowing caftan, gives them a dreamy smile and floats over in their direction.

'Did she say Teddie Spargo?' says Julie to Nadine. 'Is she related to Andy?'

Nadine's face is tight and unhappy. 'No,' she says bitterly. 'She's his *wife*.'

'They just got married a few months ago,' says Ryan. 'Poor old Nads. She's in *lurve* with Andy. When she got home from boarding school and found out he'd got married — well, poor old Nads.'

'You're a *pig*, Ryan,' says Nadine fiercely, and stalks away.

'Oh, dear,' says Julie. 'Should I go after her?'

'She's got to get over it,' says Ryan. 'No point mooning round after someone you can't have. You've got to be realistic.'

Julie wonders if Ryan yearns for someone too. Maybe he is in *lurve* with Teddie . . . She walks over to where Teddie and Barbara are deep in conversation.

Teddie sweeps back her hair with a languid gesture. '. . . literally *no* food in the house,' she is saying. 'I was trying to explain to Mary — the girl who comes in — I wanted her to stop cooking dinner for us, she makes horrible food, just disgusting, so I want to take over. But my Pidgin is pretty lousy, well, just about non-existent actually. I asked Andy but he was no help, he only knows how to say "unload the plane" and "get out of the way". So I looked up the phrasebook and I told Mary, *no kaikai, no kaikai*, thinking that meant no cooking, right? But she must have thought I meant *no food*, because when we got home from work *all the food* was gone.' Teddie rolls her eyes dramatically. 'The cupboards were empty, the fridge, everything. We had to go to the Highlander for dinner. She *totally* misunderstood me.'

Barbara frowns. 'You need to be careful, Teddie. Give them an inch and they'll take a mile.'

'You think she did it on purpose?' says Teddie, wide-eyed.

'Oh, Teddie, of course she did! They're not stupid.'

'Well, it's my own fault,' says Teddie. 'I gave Mary the excuse.'

Nadine reappears. She says scornfully, 'You do realise that Mary isn't a name?'

'What?'

'*Meri* — it means a maid — it's not her actual *name*.'

'No!' says Teddie doubtfully. 'I'm sure her name's Mary. I can't have been calling her "Maid" all this time.'

'It means *woman*,' says Ryan. 'Actually.'

'That's even worse!' wails Teddie.

'Would you like me to have a word with her?' says Barbara. 'That might be for the best. You really can't let them —'

'Oh, that reminds me,' Teddie interrupts. 'There's a kind of do this arvo, at Colditz. A pool party, barbie kind of thing. Andy thought Ryan and Julie might like to come along.'

Nadine opens her mouth to protest, then shuts it again.

'Well,' says Barbara stiffly. 'Of course you don't want the boss hanging over you all the time. I can understand that.'

'Oh, you can come if you like!' exclaims Teddie. 'But, you know . . . you'd probably be . . . bored —'

'Why can't I go?' demands Nadine.

'It's not for kids,' says Ryan. 'There won't be lemonade and fairy bread.'

Teddie looks at him and Julie. 'So you guys are coming?'

'Sure,' shrugs Ryan. 'Why not?'

'I don't know,' says Julie. 'I'd better check with Tony.'

'Oh, he won't mind,' says Barbara. 'He'll be relieved, he was wondering how on earth he was going to keep you entertained.'

Oh.

Julie says, 'What's Colditz?'

'It's the flats where the guys live — the other HAC pilots,' says Teddie. 'It looks like a prison block.'

'Those flats are perfectly good accommodation,' says Barbara.

'How come you and Andy aren't living there, Teddie?' says Ryan.

Teddie wrinkles her nose. 'I don't know,' she says vaguely. 'Curry gave us the yellow house when I came up. He's such a sweetie . . . See you later . . .'

She waves, and melts into the crowd, with her basket boy trotting after her.

Barbara gazes after her. 'She really is the most exasperating girl. I don't know how Andy stands it . . . We rented the yellow house for them. Because we assumed there must be some reason why they got married so quickly.'

Ryan whistles. 'Up the duff?'

Nadine squeaks. 'They're having a *baby*?'

'Well, there's no sign of it,' says Barbara. 'I suppose they might have been mistaken — or she might have —' She stops. 'Anyway, I expect they will have one soon enough. There's not much else to do.'

'And we *do* make our own fun,' murmurs Ryan, so that only Julie can hear.

'It's not fair,' says Nadine. 'I never get to do *anything*.'

'I could walk you round to Colditz, if you like,' Ryan says to Julie. 'It's not far.'

'Okay — thanks.' Caroline told her not to bother bringing her bathers, because Tony lived so far from the sea. Had she thrown them in, after that last repack, or not? She can't remember.

'So, Mum, Mum, can I have that puppy?' asks Nadine.

'*No*, darling! We've already got Roxy, and you've got enough pets, you only get to see them for six weeks a year anyway! And those poor little pups are *racked* with disease.'

Julie follows them back to the car, nursing her bilum of fruit in her arms.

'Should be a good do, this arvo,' says Ryan. 'The Colditz guys are pretty cool.'

Julie wonders fleetingly if Simon Murphy might be there ... But already, somehow, she knows that he won't be.

6

When Teddie said *pool party*, Julie had visions of a palm-lined, turquoise swimming pool, like something out of Hollywood. When she arrives at Colditz with Ryan and the Spargos, and sees the canvas-sided tub of lukewarm water, filled with a garden hose, she feels hot and foolish.

A knot of shirtless young men stand around the homemade barbecue, beers in hand. There is one young woman in the pool, in a crochet bikini, her hair dangling in wet strings, her skin as golden as a goddess's. The men around her gaze at her with the same drooling eagerness as the boys around the barbecue, poking hopefully at the meat. Julie tries not to stare, torn between envy and scorn. A couple of other girls sprawl on the grass, careless and loose-limbed, but they are far outnumbered by the men.

If I can't find a boyfriend here, there really is no hope.

Andy strips off his shirt and leaps into the water with a whoop. But Teddie and Ryan head for the shade beneath the trees, and Julie follows them. The thought of exposing her pale, skinny body beside the golden goddess is too humiliating. Teddie smiles vaguely around, behind her dark glasses and big hat. Ryan drops onto his stomach and starts plucking up blades of grass with his usual scowl.

Neither of them seems inclined to conversation, so Julie eavesdrops on the group slouching in deckchairs nearby. They are discussing Independence, though from the way they speak, they might be talking about impending Armageddon.

'It won't be safe to stay. We'll all be murdered in our beds. They're getting cheekier already. Did you hear the *raskols* roaring up and down Wahgi Parade last night?'

'As soon as the *kiaps* pull out, there'll be nothing to stop them from slaughtering each other. It'll be full-scale tribal warfare.'

'They'll kick us all out. This time next year, there won't be any Europeans left, apart from the God-botherers.'

'It's the end of an era . . . It'll never be the same.'

It's odd, Julie thinks. There is anger in the way they speak, bitter resentment at their dismissal from the scene. But there is a wistfulness too, nostalgia for the lives they are still leading, as if they see themselves as ghosts already; they miss living here and they haven't even left yet. Did the Romans sit around talking like this, before their empire fell?

'Hey, Ryan, what's Curry going to do? Stay here or go *finis*?'

Ryan shrugs and mumbles. 'If it was up to Dad, we'd stay here forever. But I'm pretty sure Mum wants to go home.'

Julie leans forward. 'If your family leaves — what would happen to the company?'

Andy throws himself down on the grass, scattering drops of water over them all. 'Don't worry about Mac, Juliet. Someone'll give your dad a job, whatever happens. He's the best pilot I've ever met.'

'Really?' Julie feels an unexpected glow of pride in the stranger who is her father. 'Andy? Can I ask you something?'

'Sure thing, Juliet. But let me remind you that I'm a married man.'

She ignores this, embarrassed. She says, 'Why aren't there any local people here? Any nationals?'

Andy's grin fades. He shifts his body uneasily on the grass. 'Well, I guess we just don't make friends with many of the nationals. There's not much chance to, you know . . . mingle.'

'But you must meet some local people.'

Andy laughs. 'Well, yeah. There's our meri, there are the *kago bois* at work. But they'd hardly fit in here, would they?' He waves his hand vaguely at the gathering around them.

Ryan says patiently, 'You don't understand, Julie. It's all separate. They stick to their people, and we stick to ours. It's just more comfortable that way.'

'But you must have local friends,' Julie says 'You grew up here. Didn't you go to school with local kids?'

'Not really. The schools are in two streams, the A stream for the expats, and the T stream for the nationals. They get taught in Pidgin, and the expat kids get taught in English. Makes sense when you think about it.'

'But —' Julie stops. Andy and Ryan are looking at her indulgently, as if she is a bit dim for even asking the question. And it does make sense to teach the locals in their own language. And you couldn't teach Australian kids in Pidgin. So maybe it is the only way —

Teddie, who has been staring at the sky and not apparently listening to any of this, suddenly returns to earth. 'Are we doing anything tomorrow? How about a picnic by the river? You're not going to church or anything, are you, Julie?'

'God, no!' she says, and everyone laughs, though she didn't mean to be funny.

'Better make it early,' says Andy. 'Before the rain comes.'

*

The next day Julie is squashed in with Teddie in the back of Andy's little green Datsun, bumping along a bush road after the Crabtrees' blue Holden. It doesn't take long to leave all signs of the town behind; after only a few minutes, it's as if they've plunged into the ancient past, a world of villages and garden plots and uncleared jungle.

Andy pulls up by the banks of a shallow, clear-flowing stream. The Crabtrees and Roxy the dog spill from the other car, and soon Barbara is spreading rugs over the sandy bank and unpacking eskies of beer and sandwiches. Tony and Julie have brought nothing. 'Don't worry about it,' he'd shrugged. 'Barb always handles the catering.'

Julie knows her mother would be horrified if she could see that her daughter had turned up to a picnic empty-handed. But Caroline is a long way away.

The river is as clear as liquid glass. The stones at the bottom are honey-coloured, amber, with silken threads of sunlight flickering over them through the water. Birds call in the trees, but their songs are unfamiliar. There is one with a long whistle, followed by a questioning trill, and another with a cascade of notes like a waterfall. The trees are so thickly crowded, it's impossible to imagine walking between them. The road is close by, but there is almost no traffic. They might have been the last humans on the planet, or explorers on an undiscovered continent. The only sounds are the songs of the birds, and their own voices.

Nadine says, 'Let's walk along the river.'

She and Ryan kick off their shoes and leave them on the rocks. Julie tugs off her sandals and wades into the ankle-deep water, so icy it makes her gasp. Her toes waver whitely underwater, like carved marble.

Nadine steps from rock to rock, as sure-footed as a cat. Julie splashes clumsily behind her; Ryan brings up the rear, stumping through the water with his hands shoved in his pockets, his shoulders hunched. Without speaking, the three of them in a silent line, they make their way upstream, around bends, across gurgling rapids, through a knee-deep pool of beer-coloured water, lined with soft mud, until they've left the adults far behind. There is not one piece of litter, not one soft drink can or scrap of plastic. The sun pours out its gentle warmth onto their skin. The birds sing, the breeze murmurs in the trees.

On the way back, Ryan, behind Nadine's oblivious back, stretches out his hand toward Julie's. She has a split second to decide: is this something she wants?

Oh, well, she thinks, it can't hurt. And I can always get out of it later.

She reaches out her hand and catches hold of his, and without looking at each other, they splash along side by side, their hands clasped.

When they come in sight of the others, sitting on the bank, and Roxy snuffling on the rocks, Ryan lets her hand fall. And for the rest of the afternoon, they both pretend that nothing has happened.

Midway through the picnic lunch, Julie notices that Nadine is struggling to stifle a fit of giggles. She feels a prickle of anxiety. Had Nadine noticed her and Ryan holding hands? She says, 'What's the joke?'

'You —' Nadine can hardly speak. 'You and Tony!'

'What?'

Tony and Julie exchange a nervous look.

'The way you eat your sandwiches!' crows Nadine. 'Nibble, nibble, nibble all along the crust, and then you throw the crusts away! You both do it exactly the same! It's so funny!'

Tony gazes down, bewildered, at the crust at his hand. Julie, scarlet-faced, tries to scrunch up her discarded crusts in the sandwich paper. Then they catch each other's eye, and Tony gives his shy smile.

'Never did like crusts,' says Tony.

'Me either,' admits Julie.

Nadine shouts, 'You even have the same smile! Look, look at them! They've both got the same dimple!'

'Shut up, Nads,' says Ryan. 'Can't you see you're embarrassing them?'

'It's okay,' says Julie. 'I don't mind.'

Tony looks away. His cheeks are flushed with pink, but Julie thinks he's pleased.

'You're coming over tomorrow, right?' says Nadine anxiously, before Julie and Tony go home that night.

Julie doesn't look at Ryan but she can feel his eyes burning on her.

'Yeah,' she says. 'Okay, I will.' And Ryan's whole body relaxes.

*

The next morning, after Tony leaves for work, Julie is moving sluggishly around the unit, preparing to walk around to the Crabtrees' house, when she hears a knock on the door. She assumes it's Ryan, come to escort her, so she unlocks the door without checking.

But it's a woman standing on the doorstep, a national — a girl, really, not much older than Julie is. She is holding a bilum filled with lemons.

'*Yu baim muli, misis?*'

She smiles at Julie, but her eyes are pleading, almost desperate. She offers up her bag of lemons, and Julie sees that her meri blouse is ragged, gaping open with a tear beneath the arm, and her baggy skirt is grimy and faded.

68

'*Muli?*'

'Yes!' says Julie. 'Yes, I'll buy some. Wait a minute.'

She runs back to the bedroom and rummages in her shoulder bag for her purse. She can hear Barbara's admonishing voice in her head: *don't leave them on the step with the door open, they could run in and help themselves* . . . She pushes the voice away.

'I'll have two — no, threepela,' she says, and holds up three fingers, just in case. The girl opens the bilum to let her choose, and Julie gives her a ten cent coin. She knows from the market that it's far too much for a few lemons. 'Take it,' she says. 'Please.'

The girl lowers her eyes and slips the coin inside her clothes. Maybe she can't believe her luck. She's hurrying away — probably afraid that Julie will change her mind — when Julie does call her back.

'Wait a sec — do you want some of these?' She tears open the bundle of old clothes that Barbara gave her for the missionaries next door. She pulls out a dress, a T-shirt, a yellow blouse. 'You want them? For you, look.'

The girl steps back, shaking her head uncertainly. But as Julie waves the clothes at her, insisting, 'For you. You take them!' she creeps forward again, and at last she accepts the dress. Julie beams; then she has her inspiration.

'You want a job? Work? Work here?'

Tony has no meri. Julie can help this girl, help her in a lasting way: she can give her a job. Then she won't need to tramp from door to door, flogging lemons. Julie can help her.

'You be our meri? Cleanim house? Cookim food? Kaikai?' She is laughing at her own pitiful attempt at Pidgin, and the girl giggles too. 'What's your name?' says Julie. 'Name belong you?' She points at herself. 'I'm Julie. Julie.' She points at the girl. 'You?'

The girl whispers so softly that Julie has to lean forward to catch it. 'Lina.'

'Okay! Lina! Will you be our meri? Yes? Okay —' Julie realises she'd better let Tony know what's happening. 'You come back tomorrow?'

The girl nods, and clutching her bag of lemons, she scurries off down the driveway. Julie gazes after her, not sure how well she'd managed to make herself understood. But she is well-pleased, and proud of herself, as she marches around to the Crabtrees' house.

'Oh, dear.' Barbara passes a hand across her eyes. 'You don't know anything about this girl! If you wanted a meri, you should have asked me to find someone reliable, one of Koki's *wontoks* ... And Tony's always said he doesn't want a meri.'

'Well, maybe he's changed his mind,' says Julie stubbornly. A familiar feeling of defiance hardens inside her. Barbara and Caroline might not have much else in common, but clearly they'd agree on one thing — whatever Julie does is wrong.

But later that night, when she confesses what she's done, it seems Barbara might have been right. Tony is dismayed.

'Oh, no, I don't —' He stares at the wall. 'I don't want a meri. You should have asked me first.'

'I was only trying to help,' says Julie.

'Yeah, I know . . . I had a meri when I first came up here, but it didn't work out. Never again.'

'Okay. Sorry.'

'Apart from anything else, I can't afford it,' says Tony apologetically. 'I've got to save up for my old age, you know.'

'Okay, okay,' says Julie. 'I'll tell her to forget it. I'm sorry.'

'Don't worry about it.' Tony rubs his bald spot, running his finger along the dent of his scar. 'Look . . . I wish we could live like the Crabtrees. Big house, meri and a garden boi, all of that. But —'

'I don't want to live like the Crabtrees. I was just trying to —'

'Make my life easier?' Tony finishes the sentence for her. 'Thanks, mate. I appreciate it. But I'm doing all right. Don't worry about me.'

Julie stares at him helplessly, unable to explain that she wasn't thinking of him at all; it was Lina she'd been trying to help. And now she is going to have to turn her away, because Tony feels too poor to employ her. And yet Tony has so much more than Lina . . .

'I'm sorry, love,' says Tony.

Julie manages to muster up a smile. 'It's all right.'

Tony says, 'You want a game of backgammon? I play a game with Gibbo now and then.'

'I don't know how.'

Tony's face falls, but then Julie adds, 'Maybe you could teach me?' And the shy, eager smile spreads across his face once more.

7

'But we *always* have a Christmas party,' says Nadine, a few days after the picnic by the river.

'Not this year,' says Barbara.

'But why not? We *always* —'

'I just don't feel up to it this year. I've done it for seventeen years. Let someone else do the work for a change.'

'Teddie and Andy are going to have a Christmas party,' says Ryan unexpectedly from the depths of the armchair where he's curled around his guitar.

'Are they?' Barbara shoots him a look. 'Well. Good. Good for them. I hope it's a great success.'

She stalks from the room and Ryan chuckles as he pulls Julie down onto the arm of his chair. 'She's pissed off now. She makes out she doesn't want to do the work, but she doesn't want to lose the glory either. Poor Mum.' His arm snakes around Julie's waist and he presses his face against her back.

'Yay!' Nadine jumps up. 'Now I have to figure out what to wear. Come and help, Julie.'

Julie wriggles out of Ryan's embrace. 'Just for a minute,' she says apologetically. 'Girl stuff.'

Ryan scowls and strums a chord. 'Don't take too long.'

*

Two nights later, Julie walks with tentative steps into fairyland. Teddie and Andy's garden glows with Chinese lanterns of scarlet paper, and garlands of white flowers looped between the trees. Soft music and golden light stream from the windows, echoing the tangerine flush of the declining sun.

Julie is the first to arrive, because the Spargos' house is just two doors up from Tony's. Her father rang, mid-afternoon, from the HAC terminal. 'Looks like I'll be stuck here for a while, mate. If I'm not back in time for Andy's Christmas whatsit, don't wait for me, you go along and I'll meet you there. You'll be right, won't you?'

Julie said it didn't matter, that she didn't mind at all, but as she picks her way up the Spargos' steep driveway, she wishes she'd stayed at the Crabtrees' house after all, and arrived with them. Even though she's wearing her best party dress, and a necklace borrowed from Nadine, there is something forlorn about arriving at a party alone.

Teddie draws her inside. 'I'm *glad* you're early. Come and sit on the bed while I put my face on.'

Julie follows her into the bedroom, feeling suddenly childish in her pale blue floaty dress. Teddie is wearing a tight, high-collared Chinese dress of creamy silk, her long copper hair knotted at the nape of her neck. Julie can't stop staring at her, wondering how such a demure outfit can be so incredibly sexy. She catches sight of herself in Teddie's dressing-table mirror, her hair hanging loose on her shoulders, and feels disconsolate. Her light-brown hair is messy and limp; it's nothing hair. Nothing colour, nothing length. Maybe she should just cut it all off.

'Hey, Juliet!' calls Andy from the kitchen. 'No Mac? What have you done with him?'

'He's still at work, with Curry. He said to come without him.'

Julie perches gingerly on Teddie and Andy's unmade bed while Teddie sweeps a cotton ball languidly across her face. Andy pokes his head round the door and whistles.

'Wow, Juliet, you look gorgeous.'

Julie murmurs something, flushing, but he's still talking. 'Guess who I ran into in town? That guy Simon, the one we flew up from Moresby. You two seemed to hit it off, so I invited him to come along tonight; I thought you might like to see him again.'

'Oh!' Julie twists around on the bed to face him. 'Do you think he'll come?'

75

'Of course he will.' Teddie dusts her nose with powder. 'It's a *party*.'

Julie wants to ask, *did he mention me*? But she can't. Her face feels hot. Andy leans back in the doorway. 'I thought it was interesting what you were saying the other day, about us not having any friends among the nationals. It does seem a bit ridiculous when you think about it. So I hope he comes, too. Should be interesting, anyway.'

'I'm glad you asked him,' says Julie, though she isn't exactly sure if Simon Murphy counts as a national.

Teddie surveys her face critically in the mirror. A cloud of faint perfume hangs in the air. Julie breathes in cautiously. Her mother believes in the natural look; she doesn't often use make-up, and Julie doesn't often use it either.

Teddie says, 'Would you like me to do you, too, when I'm finished?'

'Oh! I don't usually —'

'Go on, let me, I love doing it. I always thought I'd like to be a make-up artist, you know, for TV, or films.' She sweeps a deft stroke of eyeliner beneath each eye. 'Not much scope for that, up here, except when the Drama Club puts on a play. So you should let me practise, to keep my hand in.'

'Well, if it's doing you a favour . . .' Suddenly Julie is desperate for Teddie to transform her into a movie star.

'If you don't let her, she'll practise on me.' Andy grins and disappears.

'Your turn.' Teddie sits Julie at the dressing table and sets to work.

When she's finished, Julie can feel the mask of foundation on her skin, smoothing away her spots and freckles, the sweep of mascara heavy on her lashes; she can taste the lipstick on her mouth. She stares at the unfamiliar reflection in the glass, a smoky-eyed, pale-lipped girl.

'Your eyes are quite pretty, actually,' says Teddie dispassionately. 'I love hazel eyes, you can bring out all sorts of colours in them. Now, one more thing . . .' She twists Julie's hair up onto the top of her head and jabs it with pins, then teases out two wispy curls to frame her face. 'Perfect.'

The gold necklace at her throat glints as Julie turns her face this way and that. She doesn't look like herself any more; it's a relief.

Julie steps out into the garden, feeling like a princess entering an enchanted kingdom. The brief Highland dusk gathers softly in the corners of the yard, the lanterns glow from the trees. Andy has set up a table with a bucket of punch, and Julie helps herself to a paper cup of the sweet, fruity brew. *Just one cup*, she argues with the phantom of her mother, *it's a party*.

'Juliet!' Andy wolf-whistles as she shyly twirls in front of him, and he seems to really mean it this time. He takes a drag of a cigarette, then holds it out to her. She shakes her head. 'Sure?' he says. 'It's hand-grown.'

She smiles vaguely, thinking of the sheaves of tobacco at the market; then she smells the sweet smoke. 'Is that from Gibbo's garden?'

Andy laughs, and shakes his head, refusing to answer. A gang of rowdy pilots from Colditz arrives, and they swarm over the garden. Clutching her paper cup, Julie retreats. She bumps into Gibbo, who materialises like a wraith at her shoulder.

'Silence is a friend who never betrays,' he says.

Julie nods, and gulps, and edges around the side of the house. The front garden looks out over the street from the top of the hill. Three spindly gum trees stand sentinel along the fence of bamboo stakes. Teddie and Andy haven't decorated out here; perhaps they ran out of paper lanterns. Julie leans her elbows on the fence and stares at the primary school across the road. She can see it from Tony's place too, but because the Spargos live at the top of the hill, the view is clearer here.

'That's my old school.'

Julie turns and there is Simon Murphy. Her heart gives a skip. He comes to stand beside her at the fence, and in the fading light he points out one building, raised

78

on stilts, by itself on one side of the grounds. 'That was my building, the A stream building.'

'So you were in the A stream? They told me that was just for —' Julie skids to a halt.

'Just for expats?' Simon looks her directly in the eye. 'You don't have to be European. If you speak English at home, you can go into the A stream. It's just that not many Highlanders qualify.'

'But you do. Obviously . . .'

'Obviously,' he says dryly. 'My father's Australian. Irish-Australian. My mother was born in the village. I can speak her *plestok* — her tribal language, Pidgin, and English. Oh, and I did some French at school. But that's pretty rusty now.'

'Are you at uni now?' Julie grabs eagerly to change the subject.

Simon gives a deep sigh. 'I'm supposed to be on holidays. But I don't think I'll go back. Dad's not getting any younger. He hasn't said anything, but I think it's time I learned how to manage Keriga so I can take over when the time comes.' He raps the fence. 'Touch wood, he's got a good few years left. He's a tough old bastard. 'Scuse my French.'

'Could I come and visit your coffee plantation some time? I've never seen a plantation; it sounds so romantic.'

Simon laughs. 'Nothing romantic about it. Just bloody hard work.' He leans on the fence so he's half-turned toward her. It's almost dark now, she can hardly see him; he's just a voice in the shadows. He says proudly, 'My father was one of the first Europeans to come into the Highlands, back in the nineteen-thirties. He arrived just after the Leahy brothers.'

'Wow,' says Julie respectfully, and makes a mental note to ask Tony who the Leahy brothers were. Maybe they're related to the Leyland Brothers who have that cheesy TV show . . .

'Dad's never been back to Australia,' says Simon. 'Not even to visit me at school. He loves this place. God's own country, he calls it.'

'Is that why he married your mum?'

'Well,' says Simon after a moment. 'They didn't exactly get married.'

Julie's cheeks burn. 'Well,' she says at last. 'My parents didn't *stay* married — so that's kind of the same thing, isn't it?'

'Your name's McGinty, isn't it. Sounds as if you're Irish, too.'

Julie feels caught out. 'I don't know. I don't know anything about Tony's family. We've only just met, really. He and my mother split up when I was little, and he came up here. This is the first time I've visited him.'

'You don't know *anything* about your people, about where you've come from?' Simon sounds shocked. 'That must be rough.' His voice is so gentle, she realises that he feels genuinely sorry for her.

Suddenly the darkness makes it easy to talk to him; or perhaps it's the punch. She says, 'It must be rough for you, too. Caught in the middle.'

Simon is silent for a moment. 'Sometimes,' he says. 'But in a way I feel lucky, you know? I've got the best of both worlds.'

'My mother thinks I should change my name,' Julie tells him. 'She's gone back to her maiden name, and now she wants me to take it, too.'

'But you'd rather keep your dad's name?'

'It's not that so much. But I *can't* take her name.'

'Why not?'

She lowers her voice. 'It's . . . Dooley.'

They both laugh. Julie feels a sudden sharp pang of homesickness for her mum, for their empty house, for the beach, for her friends — but then, like a cloud crossing the face of the moon, it passes away. She stands next to Simon in the darkness, not speaking, but comfortable in the silence. At their backs, the noise of the party is building steadily: music, laughter, the clink of glasses, all wrapped into a muffled roar. Above their heads, the stars are beginning to wink into the velvet sky.

Simon says in a low voice, 'Did you make your friend invite me tonight? You can tell me the truth. I want to know.'

'No,' says Julie honestly. 'It was nothing to do with me. He just ran into you and he thought — he thought you might like to come.'

'I don't normally get invited to this kind of thing. My social life took a bit of a hit after the primary school birthday parties dried up.'

'Well, that's crazy.'

'Yes. It is.'

'I'm glad you came,' says Julie impulsively. 'Andy and Teddie —'

'*There* you are! What are you doing hiding back here?'

It's Ryan Crabtree, storming out from round the corner of the house. He grabs her hand. 'I've been looking for you everywhere! I thought you hadn't come, I nearly went down to Tony's to see if you were still dressing up or something. Come on, I want to get a beer.'

Julie is pretty sure he's already had at least one. She pulls her hand from his. 'Ryan, this is my friend Simon Murphy — Simon, this is Ryan Crabtree . . .'

'It's all right, Julie, we know each other,' says Simon. 'We were at school together, weren't we, Ryan?'

'Yeah,' mumbles Ryan. 'Yeah, Simon was two grades ahead of me. How's it going, mate?'

'Had a year at uni, but I'm thinking I might come back and work at Keriga, learn how to take over. What are you up to?'

'Still got a year of school to go.' Ryan shuffles his feet. 'Mum and Dad are making noises about uni, too — engineering, maybe.'

Julie says, 'I thought you wanted to be a musician, Ryan?'

'Yeah, well, maybe, we'll see.' The quick annoyance in his voice tells Julie that she's betrayed a secret. 'C'mon, Jules, let's get a drink.'

He drags her back around the house and grabs a stubby of South Pacific from an esky.

'Are you supposed to have that?'

'Come on, Julie, it's a *party*. It's *Christmas*. Loosen up.'

He sloshes more punch into her paper cup, and before she knows it, they're dancing. The magical canopy of the rotary clothesline stretches above them, threaded with streamers, with gashes of star-sprinkled sky beyond. They dance close, not touching, but close enough that Julie can feel his hot breath on her cheek, her ear. The tendril of hair brushes her neck. She gulps her punch and lets the music sway through her.

'I should go and talk to Simon — I feel bad running off like that,' she calls into Ryan's ear at the end of the song.

'Relax! It's not your problem. He'll find someone else to talk to, you don't have to babysit him. He's a big boy. He took the risk of coming; he can look after himself. His choice.' Ryan puts his mouth boldly close to her ear and whispers, 'You look great tonight.'

Julie tries to look over her shoulder to check if Simon has drifted back into the side garden, the centre of the party, but she can't see him. Ryan whoops as a faster, rockier song comes on the stereo, and he grabs her hands, her cup goes flying, spilling a spray of punch across the grass, and they dance, and she forgets about Simon.

The music swirls, the stars turn, Julie kicks off her sandals and the grass is damp with dew and soft beneath her tender soles, her head spinning, the taste of punch sweet on her tongue, and the shadow of Ryan tethered to her side, Ryan's hand reaching for hers, Ryan's eyes locked on her face, just as if she were beautiful. When the lights snuff out and the music abruptly breaks off, the garden plunges into black, and groans and jeers ring out.

'Bloody power failure!'

'Useless bastards!'

Teddie drifts about with candles and a cigarette lighter, slender as a fire fairy, and Andy produces a guitar from somewhere and perches on the edge of the concrete laundry trough to strum and sing. Everyone

84

laughs, and Julie laughs too, because everyone else is laughing. And Ryan seizes her hands and pulls her into a dark corner of the garden, sheltered by a passionfruit vine, and pushes his mouth hungrily onto hers.

It's her first kiss. Her blood fizzes. Her hands creep to his face, the soft stubble of his jaw, his warm skin. His arms wrap around her, pressing her into his body. Are they hidden, or do Teddie's candles betray them?

Julie pushes Ryan's hands gently from her waist and turns her face aside. 'Okay, okay,' she murmurs. Her face feels smeared, her lips swollen. Has Simon seen them? She wants him to be watching, but if he's seen them, she will die. 'Wait, wait,' she whispers against Ryan's butting mouth. 'I just need to —' She breaks away.

Ryan pulls her back against him. 'Don't disappear.'

'I'll come back,' she promises. 'I'll be back in a minute.'

She tears herself away and slips along the fence, around the shadowy fringe of the party, toward the other side of the house. The night air is cool against her flushed face. The three spindly trees are silhouetted against the starry sky, a thicket of bamboo rustles by the water tank, like some lumbering, half-asleep beast. *My first kiss, my first kiss*. Under the New Guinea moon . . . She touches her lips with her fingertips.

'Simon? Are you there?'

Someone giggles in the dense shadow beside the house. The scent of sweet smoke drifts across the grass. 'No one here except us, darling.'

'Sorry, sorry —'

Julie stumbles away. He's gone.

'Real knowledge,' breathes a sudden voice out of the darkness, 'is to know the extent of one's ignorance.' Tombstone teeth gleam, like a skull's smile, leering up out of the night.

Julie yelps. 'Gibbo! You scared me!'

'Sorry, love,' says Gibbo, and he vanishes, folding back into the dark like a bat.

Julie leans against the wall, her heart hammering. Simon has gone. But Tony must be here somewhere, by now. Soon it will be time to go home, and leave Ryan behind. And deep down, Julie knows she is slightly relieved. She raises her fingers to her lips. Is it weird to feel that thinking about being kissed — anticipating it, then reliving it afterwards — is more fun than the actual kissing?

She can see Ryan, swimming through the wavering candlelight, looking for her. She touches her upswept hair, her floaty dress, and all at once she feels unsure of who she is. Who is Ryan searching for — Princess Juliet, spun into existence by Teddie and Andy? Or plain Julie McGinty? Would Ryan have kissed plain Julie McGinty?

She stands by the fence, wrapping darkness around her like a cloak, and watches, waiting to be found.

8

When Lina failed to show up on the morning after Julie offered her the job, Julie had felt guiltily relieved. The problem was solved without her having to do anything. Lina must have decided she didn't want to be a meri after all, or she'd got another job. Or something. If she didn't turn up, there's nothing Julie can do about it. She can hardly go out and search for her; she is absolved of responsibility.

But then, on the Monday morning after the Spargos' Christmas party, Lina comes back.

Julie answers a tap at the door, expecting to find Ryan on the doorstep. Instead it's Lina, smiling hopefully. Tony has already set off for work, so she will have to handle this alone.

Julie swallows. 'I'm so sorry . . . There's been a mistake. I shouldn't have offered you a job without checking first. Tony — my father — says he doesn't need a meri . . .' She's worried that Lina won't understand what she's saying, but she sees the girl's face fall, and apparently her meaning is clear enough. Without a word, Lina gathers herself and begins to turn away.

'No, wait! Hang on a minute —' Julie fumbles for her purse. The spending money that Caroline gave her has almost gone, but there's a five-dollar note still crumpled inside. 'Please — take this.'

Lina stares at the pink note as if she doesn't know what it is.

'It's for you. For your trouble. It's — it's compensation,' says Julie with sudden inspiration.

Lina nods, then flashes her a brief, shy smile. Then she tucks the money away inside her clothes and retreats. Julie shuts the door and leans against it. Five dollars is a lot of money, she tells herself; especially for a national. For five dollars, she shouldn't be feeling so rotten.

*

'Oh, dear, no,' says Barbara. 'That was the *worst* thing you could have done. She'll be back, tomorrow or the next day, with her hand out. You'll see.'

'But I had to give her something,' says Julie. 'I promised.'

'I'm sure you didn't *promise*,' says Barbara. 'And it's not as if you had anything in writing.'

'Well, no, but —' Julie stops, because Barbara is clearly not interested in continuing the discussion, and she's learned from arguments with Caroline that there's no point in trying. She wonders how, when Barbara and

Caroline's ideas about the world are so different, she can manage to disagree with both of them . . .

'Come on,' says Ryan, and he, Julie and Nadine drift out through the kitchen to the sunny patch of concrete outside the back door. Koki is already there, sitting on the ground, shelling peas into a tin basin between her knees. Ryan steals a handful and she smacks his knuckles. Julie picks up some pea pods and starts to slit them open with her thumbnail.

'*Tenkyu*,' says Koki, and adds something in Pidgin about ungrateful, lazy children, which Julie can understand without knowing a word. She and Koki grin peacefully at each other.

Nadine stretches her legs into the sun. 'Last year the Williamses were still here,' she says mournfully. 'And the Spitellis. We'd hang out with them every day . . . Now it's just us.'

Silently Julie splits the pods, and thumbs the peas into the basin, aware of herself as a poor substitute for the missing Williams and Spitelli clans.

Nadine sighs. 'What about Monopoly?'

Ryan ignores her. He nudges Julie's foot with his own. 'Want to go for a bike ride?'

'But we've only got two bikes,' says Nadine.

'Julie can ride yours. No one said you were invited, squirt. This excursion is for Julie and I.'

Julie and me, thinks Julie automatically. She says, 'We could go for a walk. That way Nads can come too.' Secretly she is quite happy to have Nadine along as a chaperone. She knows if they were alone, Ryan would try to kiss her again, even on bicycles, and while it's pleasant to think that he wants to, she's not completely sure that *she* wants to. Julie shifts uncomfortably on her bottom. It's never like this in books . . .

'Yeah, let's go for a walk. We can bring Roxy!' says Nadine, brightening.

Ryan shrugs. 'All right. But if you bring the dog, you look after her, okay? If she gets off the lead, I'm not chasing after her. If she ends up in someone's cooking pot, it's your problem.'

'You're a pig, Ryan,' says Nadine. 'No, you're not. Pigs are lovely. You're a — a warthog.'

Julie looks at Ryan. 'They don't really eat dogs?'

Ryan frowns and motions her to shush. From inside the house, through an open window, comes a muffled noise of banging drawers and slammed doors. 'What's Mum up to? Rearranging the furniture again?'

Nadine sits up, suddenly alert, like a rabbit who senses a hawk overhead.

The rapid *clack-clack* of Barbara's heels crosses the parquetry. Inside the kitchen, she calls, 'Koki! *Yu kam hariap!* Can I speak to you for a minute, please?'

Koki rolls her eyes, climbs laboriously to her feet, and shuffles inside. The screen door bangs behind her. Julie pulls the basin closer and continues shelling the peas. From inside the kitchen comes the sound of Barbara's raised, querulous voice, and a low, protesting murmur from Koki. Julie sees Nadine and Ryan exchange a worried glance.

Nadine scrambles to her feet. 'I'm going to find out what's going on —'

Ryan lays a restraining hand on her arm. 'Hang on —'

They all sit tensed, as if waiting for a signal, while the voices rise and fall in the kitchen. At last Nadine can bear it no longer. She shakes off Ryan's hand and rushes inside.

Julie looks at Ryan. 'Should we —?'

Slowly he climbs up. 'I guess.' He looks worried.

Julie follows him inside. Barbara is standing in the centre of the kitchen, flicking impatiently at her lighter, a cigarette balanced at the corner of her lip. Koki is nowhere to be seen.

'What happened?' Nadine cries.

Barbara finally succeeds in getting her cigarette lit. 'Nothing for you kids to worry about.' She tosses the lighter onto the table.

Ryan frowns. 'Where's Koki?'

'Gone.'

'What do you mean, gone?'

'I've sacked her.'

'*What?*'

Nadine gasps as if she's drowning, then bursts into noisy tears. 'You can't sack Koki!'

'Well, I have.' Barbara flicks a glance in Julie's direction, annoyed to have a witness to this private family drama.

'But what *for?*'

'Stealing,' says Barbara crisply. 'My gold necklace is missing from my jewellery box.'

Julie and Nadine's eyes meet in horror. 'Mum, I . . . I gave . . .' Nadine stammers.

'I think I've got it,' says Julie at the same instant.

Barbara's gaze narrows. 'Pardon?'

'Nadine lent it to me for the party . . .'

'I said Julie could borrow it . . .'

The girls speak over each other.

'It's at home,' says Julie. 'I meant to bring it back today, but — I forgot.'

Ryan whistles softly. 'Jeez, Mum, you've really stuffed up this time.'

Barbara's face is as grey as putty beneath her make-up, but her voice is steady. 'It wasn't just the necklace. I've been turning a blind eye for a long time, but enough is enough. The necklace was the last straw.'

'But she didn't *take* the necklace!' cries Nadine in agony. 'That was *me*!'

'I should have brought it back,' says Julie. 'I'll go and get it now —'

'There's no need to be dramatic, Julie. This is Nadine's fault; she should have asked permission.'

Ryan moves toward the door. 'I'll get Koki back. She can't have got far.'

'You will not!' Barbara raps out, her voice so sharp that Julie jumps backward. Nadine stares, gulping.

'But, Mum —' Ryan begins.

'We can't possibly take her back,' says Barbara. 'We'd lose all respect. We'd look ridiculous.'

'But we love Koki!' wails Nadine.

'Don't be silly!' snaps Barbara. 'You don't *love* Koki. She's a meri, for God's sake. And we won't need a meri for much longer, if we do *go finis*.'

Ryan and Nadine say nothing. Julie wonders wildly, fleetingly, if Lina could be their new meri? But no, that wouldn't be fair to Koki . . . And anyway, Julie doesn't know how to find her.

Barbara stubs out her cigarette with a twist of her wrist. 'I'm going to lie down. I've got a splitting headache.'

After she's gone, there is silence in the kitchen.

'Well,' says Ryan at last. 'I guess I can kind of see

Mum's point. We'll look pretty weak if we go running after her. It's soft.'

'But it's my fault!' wails Nadine.

'You can't just let her go!' says Julie. 'Whatever happened to Koki being your second mother?'

Ryan shrugs, embarrassed. 'That was a long time ago. Maybe Mum's right. They don't really need her any more. Nads and I aren't even here most of the time. If we were living down south, we wouldn't dream of having a — a maid or whatever.'

Julie stares at him, appalled. Then she lifts the telephone off the bench and begins to flick through the slim directory.

Nadine is wide-eyed. 'Who are you ringing?'

'Your dad. Curry.'

Julie finds the number for Highland Air Charters and dials it, her heart thumping. As the phone at the other end begins to ring, she stares at Ryan. He won't meet her eye. 'Jeez, Julie,' he mutters. 'It's not *my* fault.'

After an eternity, there is a click on the line. A breathless voice says, 'Hello? Whoops — this is HAC . . .'

'Hi, Teddie, it's me, Julie.'

'Are you after Tony? I think he's out on a flight,' says Teddie vaguely; even Julie knows by now that Tony would be out on a flight at this time of day.

'Actually, I was wondering if I could speak to Allan?'

'Really? What —?'

Ryan snatches the receiver from Julie's hand. 'Teddie, this is Ryan. I need to talk to Dad. It's important.'

Julie clasps her hands. *Thank you!* she mouths soundlessly, and Ryan pulls a face that says, *you're not giving me any choice*.

Julie crosses her fingers while Ryan tells Allan the story, and Nadine wrings her hands. Her frightened eyes dart to the door, as if she expects Barbara to charge in at any moment. Julie can hear Allan Crabtree's voice all the way from the airport — a furious roar, only slightly muffled by the telephone line.

'Yep,' says Ryan. 'Okay. Uh-huh.'

At last he hangs up the receiver and lets out a long breath that puffs the lank hair off his forehead. 'Bloody hell.'

'What did Dad say?' whispers Nadine.

Ryan shrugs. 'Go and get her back. And if she won't come back, give her a month's pay and a good reference.'

'Good,' says Julie. 'Good. That's fair.'

Ryan heads for the back door. 'I'll get my bike. You okay to stay here, Jules?'

'Of course.' She puts her arm around Nadine's shoulder. 'What about that game of Monopoly?'

She speaks with bravado, but as she and Nadine shake the dice and move their tokens round the board, they are both on high alert, silently praying that Barbara will stay safely shut in her bedroom until Ryan gets back.

But when she emerges, an hour later, Ryan still hasn't returned.

'Where's Ryan?' Barbara asks at once.

Nadine swings wide, scared eyes onto Julie's face.

'He's gone to find Koki,' says Julie.

'Why?' Barbara's voice is icy.

'Allan asked him to.'

'And how did Allan find out about it?'

Julie swallows. 'I — Ryan — we told him.'

There is a silence. 'I'm not quite sure why you found it necessary to get involved,' says Barbara pleasantly. 'It's not really any of your business, is it?'

'Well, I *did* borrow —' Julie falters. 'I suppose not.'

'I know you made a mess of hiring your own meri. But there's no need to interfere with our household arrangements, is there?'

Julie stares at the Monopoly board. Then she scrapes back her chair.

'Maybe I should go.'

'Maybe you should,' says Barbara.

'But we're in the middle —' Nadine falls silent.

Julie mutters, 'Get Ryan to ring me.' Nadine nods. Julie collects her shoulder bag and walks across the living room toward the front door. The trek across the acres of parquetry, with Barbara's eyes boring into her back, is the longest walk of her life.

About an hour later, Ryan rings her at Tony's place. He mumbles into the phone, 'Can't talk long. Mum's in the next room.'

'Did you get Koki back?'

'Yeah, I told her it was all a big mistake and we wanted her to come back. She was pretty upset, but she finally agreed.'

'Oh, *good*.'

'Listen, I'd better go. Hey, this is a bit awkward, but you're not exactly top of the hit parade with Mum at the moment —'

'Yeah, I know.'

'So I'll come over to your place tomorrow?'

A slight pause. 'Okay.'

'Don't you want me to?'

'No, no. I mean, yes, of course I do,' she says hastily. 'I'm really glad you fixed things with Koki.'

'See you tomorrow then.'

Julie hangs up, swings her feet onto the threadbare couch, and squeezes her hands between her knees. All day here, with Ryan, with no Nadine or Barbara or Tony or Koki to chaperone. Just the two of them, in an empty house. An empty house with beds and a couch and a shag-pile rug . . .

Of course she doesn't have to do anything she doesn't want to. Caroline has drummed that into her. But why doesn't she want to? Ryan is a nice boy. Nice enough. He won't try to force her. They'll just kiss.

A whole day of kissing. That will be — nice.

Julie swings herself off the couch and goes to search the kitchen for dinner ingredients. It might be a while before they're invited round to the Crabtrees' house again.

9

Julie is taking a bag of rubbish down to the incinerator when she sees Robyn in the next-door garden.

'Hey there, honey!' calls Robyn. 'You got time for that coffee now?'

Julie hesitates. Ryan is supposed to be coming over this morning. 'Okay,' she says. 'Why not.'

Inside Robyn and Graham's house, Julie stares curiously around the living room. It's crowded with family photographs, knick-knacks and embroidered mats. 'That's my hobby.' Robyn picks one up to show her the stitching. 'I order the yarns and patterns from back home, from a catalogue.'

Julie picks up a stuffed baby crocodile and tests its tiny teeth on her finger. 'Ow!' Hastily she sets it down. The crocodile stares up balefully with its small glass eyes.

Robyn produces a plate of biscuits and two mugs of coffee. 'Have you been keeping yourself busy, honey? I know there's not much for young people to do with themselves here.'

'Mm.' Julie sips. 'I guess . . .'

Robyn blinks through her wire-rimmed glasses. 'Say, how would you like to come out to the village with me today? I'm helping out at the clinic, you could give us a hand if you'd like.'

'Thanks,' says Julie. 'I'd like to see a village. But — you should know, I'm not really a Christian. I'm kind of an atheist, actually.'

'Why, that's okay, honey. I guess it's not contagious.' Robyn pushes a handful of pamphlets across the table. Julie flicks through them quickly, embarrassed. *Are You Saved? The Word: Our Lighthouse. What Does Heaven Look Like?*

'You can keep those, honey. We've got plenty.'

'Um . . . thanks.' Julie shoves them under her elbow. She says, 'Don't you feel weird —' She's not sure how to express it. 'Don't you feel weird, taking away their culture?'

'Oh, sweetie, before the missionaries arrived, they were tearing themselves apart. Tribal fighting, cannibalism, wife-beating. Oh, no, I'm not sorry at all.'

'But there must have been some good things. Their own religion, their myths?'

'Oh, there have been plenty of anthropologists to record all that,' says Robyn complacently. 'There are libraries full of books about it.'

'But if they stop believing in it, if they believe in Jesus instead, then their own religion's just — dead.'

Robyn tilts her head like a bright-eyed bird. 'The way I look at it, we're giving them something so much better than what they've lost. We're giving them the Way, the Truth and the Life. Seems like a good bargain to me, eternal life for a few stories.'

She smiles at Julie, suddenly steely, and Julie looks away. Robyn takes a biscuit and bites into it with small, even teeth. 'Anyways, it could never last. The old ways started to fall apart the minute white men walked over these mountains. As soon as the Leahy brothers and the patrol officers and the rest arrived in these valleys — why, it was all over. Guns and planes and radios . . . the twentieth century meets the Stone Age! Imagine!' She shakes her head. 'So much poverty,' she sighs. 'So much work to do.' She pushes back her chair. 'You ready, honey?'

'Can I use your phone?'

Ryan is grumpy when she tells him she's going out with Robyn to visit a village. 'What do you want to do that for? It'll be dirty and smelly and boring.'

Bugger you, thinks Julie as she hangs up. *And I'm trying so hard to be nice to you . . .* Maybe she shouldn't be trying quite so hard.

The village is perched along the spine of a ridge.

'You'd think they'd build it closer to the creek, down in the valley,' says Julie.

'It's easier to defend, up on the ridge,' says Robyn. 'That's one of the things we preach against, the tribal warfare.' She shakes her head. 'It maybe wasn't so bad when they fought with spears and bows and arrows, but now they have machetes, and sometimes guns . . . Although the *haus sik* is there now, if anyone is really badly hurt, the hospital. Did you hear about the hospital fire a couple of years back?'

Julie only half-listens as Robyn tells her the story of how some disgruntled nationals had set the hospital ablaze. Robyn doesn't seem to know exactly why they were disgruntled; it was just something that happened, inexplicable native behaviour.

Julie gazes at the grass huts, the neat gardens, the rich red soil. The huts are more substantial than she expected, real houses, cottages really, with woven walls and roofs of thick thatch. In the garden plots, women dig with sharpened sticks, while a troop of small children run shrieking and giggling along the paths. As Robyn steps out of the car, they mob her, yelling and laughing.

'Julie, honey, this is Dr Gregory.'

The doctor is a small, nervous-looking man, with thinning hair and a pointed nose, who reminds Julie of a bandicoot. Soon he and Robyn are busy in the rough, open-sided fibro building they use as a clinic, dispensing medications and bandaging wounds, with a line of patients queuing outside. Although Robyn had suggested that Julie could help out, it soon becomes plain that she doesn't know enough to give any meaningful assistance, and she is too diffident to try. She doesn't want to accidentally kill anyone.

She wanders outside, aiming her camera at the scenery rather than the people. But before long the children rush up, eager to pose and even more eager to examine the camera. She shows one little boy how to press the shutter, and poses herself with a group of kids. She can't understand their excited chatter, and she's pretty sure they can't understand her either, but they manage with sign language and face-pulling. The children drag her down to the river and put on a show for her. She makes out the word *gumi*, repeated over and over, and at last she realises that it means the inner tubes of tyres that the children ride whooping, racing each other.

The boy she'd trusted with the camera takes charge of her, leading her importantly to see the sturdy pigs, tethered by one leg, or rooting in the fallow garden plots. She sees one woman suckling a piglet at her own breast. Nadine has told her that the villagers feed piglets like this, because pigs are so valuable. *One tit for the pikininis, one for the liklik pik*, Allan said, and Barbara said, *Don't be so crude.*

Julie turns away, feeling guilty for finding the sight repulsive, but half-wishing she dared to take a photo. No one at home will believe her when she tells them; she can just imagine her friends from school, Rachel and the others, shrieking in disgust.

She eats a banana straight off the tree, and then the little boy tugs at her arm and half pushes, half pulls her inside one of the huts.

Julie has to duck to enter the low doorway. Inside, it's dark, and dense with the smell of wood smoke and grease and bodies. For a second she feels her stomach rise, but she swallows hard and the nausea passes. She blinks, and makes out a woman sitting by the fire. She greets Julie, staring down at the ground, and mutters furiously to the little boy, who whines in protesting argument.

Gazing around at the fire pit, the woven mats, the baskets, the scraps of cloth and discarded tins, Julie feels a sudden hot wave of shame, stronger than the nausea had been. What is she doing here, with a camera round her neck, invading someone's home, uninvited? She is treating the village like a wildlife sanctuary; she has no right to be here.

She murmurs an incoherent apology and ducks outside again, into the relief of the cool sweet air. She almost feels like tearing the camera from her neck and hurling it into the bushes. She stumbles away from the huts, away from the river, heading blindly along the rough path up the slope. All she cares about is getting away from the villagers, away from Robyn and the doctor; she needs to find a cool, private place where she can hide her face.

She hurries up the hill, deeper into the bush, leaving the faint noise of the river and the murmur of voices behind her. The path divides and she chooses a track at random. The trees crowd around her, the cool green silence of the bush closing in. A bird call rings out from the treetops; the leaves whisper. She stops in sudden indecision, turns around, and hurries back the way she came, or at least the way she thinks she came. But the path is still going uphill, not down; she can't hear the river any more.

Suddenly she knows she is lost.

More slowly now, she pushes her way along the track. 'Robyn? Dr Gregory? Hello?'

Her voice is thin and wavering; she clamps her mouth shut. Doggedly she walks on. This track must lead somewhere, she tells herself, to the river, or to another village.

The gold and emerald day is hushed; the beauty of it pierces her. Her heart calms, her feet slow. Sunlight dapples the path. High above the trees, a light plane drones across the sky. It might be Tony, or Andy, or Gibbo, oblivious to her, far below, hidden under the veil of leaves.

She can see the trees thinning out ahead, and she hurries on until the track emerges onto an unsealed road, wide enough to take trucks, and rutted from traffic. She halts, biting her lip, not knowing which way to walk. She looks left and right, but no one is in sight. After a moment, she turns left, which she thinks is the direction of the village, and starts to walk.

She's been walking for about ten minutes when she hears an engine behind her. Her heart starts to thud. Do raskol gangs drive round in the daytime? How can she ask for help, when she can't even remember the name of the village she was in? She'll have to ask for a lift back to Hagen . . .

A battered, mud-stained Jeep draws up beside her. The window is wound down and Simon Murphy leans across. Julie's heart somersaults.

'*Julie?* What are you doing here?'

Incoherent with relief, she starts to stammer out an explanation, but Simon cuts her short. He flings open the passenger-side door. 'Hop in.'

She climbs up, bangs the door shut, and Simon releases the handbrake so the Jeep jerks forward.

'You don't know the name of the village?'

'No.' She is shamefaced.

'But there's a clinic there? I think I've got a fair idea where you were, but it's a long way round in the Jeep.' Simon thinks for a moment. 'We're not far from Keriga. What if I take you there, we get a message to the clinic to say where you are, we can have a bite to eat, and then I'll drive you home?' He shoots her a look. 'How does that sound?'

She can't understand why he's so tentative. 'That sounds *perfect*. Thanks a *billion*.' She slumps back on her seat, weak with gratitude.

'No worries. Got to help a damsel in distress.'

'My knight in shining Jeep.'

'Hasn't been shining for a while; it could do with a wash.'

They bump along the track for a few minutes until they reach the top of a ridge, where Simon halts the Jeep, the engine still running. 'There it is.'

Julie can tell he's trying to sound matter-of-fact, but he can't suppress the pride in his voice. Keriga lies in a valley, fringed by hazy purple mountains. Simon rolls the Jeep slowly forward. 'There are the coffee bushes, can you see?'

He drives them down into the valley, among the dense deep green of the coffee bushes, and stops the Jeep.

The clusters of red and green berries gleam like miniature Christmas baubles. He tells her about the Brazilian slump, about frost, and the roller-coaster of international prices. She nods and tries to look intelligent. He hails a pair of men strolling between the rows of bushes, and introduces them to Julie as Moses, the foreman, and one of the workers, Ezra. He speaks to them in Pidgin, and they grin and shuffle as they reply. Ezra nods and saunters off; Simon calls sharply to him, and Ezra breaks into a trot. Julie realises with a shock that Simon is effectively their boss, though he's at least ten years younger than they are.

'I've sent Ezra to the clinic, to tell them where you are. Did you still want to have a look round?'

'Yes, please.'

In one of the drying sheds, he shows her an open sack of raw beans. She runs her fingers through the loose grey kernels, each bean rustling and light as parchment. She plunges her arm deep into the sack, and the dense mass of the beans drags at her like quicksand until she tugs free. The beans don't smell like coffee; the magical oil is trapped, hidden until roasting, called out by the power of fire. She asks Simon if she can keep a few beans, as a souvenir, and he pours a handful into a paper bag.

'Come up to the house,' he says. 'You must be starving. It's way after lunchtime.'

The house is shabby, dark and rambling, surrounded by lush flowering gardens. Simon steps up onto the verandah and calls out for his mother. 'I've brought someone for lunch!'

Julie is pleased to be described as a lunch guest, rather than a lost child picked up by the side of the road. She tries to arrange her face to look mature and sophisticated, for meeting Simon's parents.

It's a genuine surprise when Simon's mother comes bustling out of the house to greet them, a small, comfortably plump local woman, a couple of inches shorter than Julie. Somehow Julie had forgotten that she was a New Guinean. She shakes Dulcie's hand and stammers, 'Pleased to meet you.' Dulcie holds onto Julie's hand and smiles into her eyes. Already Julie has grown used to the shy, giggling manner of the Highland women, ducking their heads and laughing behind their hands; but Dulcie has the same direct, almost challenging gaze as Simon himself. She is about forty years old, her skin smooth and unlined; her hair is mostly black, with only the odd thread of silver wire coiling at her temples.

'Are you hungry?'

'Starving,' says Julie gratefully.

Dulcie smiles. 'Mr Murphy and me, we had our lunch already.' She picks up Simon's wrist and shakes it in mock anger. 'Your watch *bagarap*?'

'Sorry I'm late, Ma,' says Simon. 'I got stuck in town.'

Dulcie rolls her eyes. 'You like sandwiches?' she asks Julie. 'Good.'

While Dulcie disappears into the kitchen to find Simon and Julie some lunch, Simon leads Julie inside.

'Julie, this is my dad. Dad, this is Julie McGinty, remember, the girl who got me a flight from Moresby?'

Again, Julie's absurdly pleased that Simon has discussed her with his father.

'Pleased to meet you, Mr Murphy.'

'Call me Patrick.'

Simon's father is a gaunt, craggy old man, with a shock of white hair, who hauls himself painfully from the depths of his chair to shake Julie's hand in a massive, bony grip.

'Julie got herself lost in the bush,' says Simon. 'I said I'd run her home after lunch. If you don't mind putting off our walk for another hour or so —'

Patrick shrugs. 'I can wait an hour. The plantation's not going anywhere.' He turns his faded blue eyes on Julie. 'Shouldn't you ring someone, and tell them you're alive? People are going to be worried about you. They've probably got the police out by now.'

'I sent Ezra with a message,' says Simon.

'Maybe I should ring — my friend. Ryan Crabtree.' She can't look at Simon; she hopes she isn't blushing.

'In case anyone is looking for me, and they contact the Crabtrees, he can tell them not to panic.'

Simon raises an eyebrow. 'Sure.'

Julie dials the Crabtrees' number from Patrick's old-fashioned study, full of dark, heavy wooden furniture. A clock ticks slowly from a bookcase. It's like stepping back in time.

'Hello?'

Thank God, it's Nadine.

'Nads? It's me, Julie. Listen, I got a bit lost today. If anyone wants to know where I am, can you tell them I'm fine and I'm coming home soon? Someone's giving me a lift back.'

'Okay.' Nadine's voice is puzzled. 'So where are you now?'

'At the Murphys' plantation, at Keriga. Simon's going to drive me home.'

'Oh!' says Nadine. 'Oh, okay.'

Julie hears a noise in the background; Nadine covers the receiver, and Julie hears her muffled voice. 'Julie — with Simon Murphy —' Nadine removes her hand. 'Julie? Do you want to talk to Ryan?'

'No, I've got to go now,' says Julie hastily. 'Tell him I'll ring when I get back, okay?'

She bangs down the phone and returns outside. Dulcie brings out a plate of sandwiches, and Julie and Simon eat them at a table on the verandah.

'Sit down, Ma,' urges Simon, but Dulcie shakes her head.

'I got too much to do.' She smiles at Julie and retreats inside.

'Oh, well,' says Simon. 'Next time, she'll stay and talk to you.'

Next time. Julie reaches for a sandwich, her heart suddenly light.

The view is spectacular, the bright green of the garden shading softly into the darker green of the coffee fields, and the misty velvet of the mountains.

'I'd better get you back to town.' Simon brushes the crumbs from his fingers. 'Everything was okay when you rang? No search parties out for you?'

'It was fine,' she says. 'I don't think anyone even noticed I was gone.'

10

'How old was your mother when the Australian explorers came? Can she remember it?' Julie asks Simon on the way back.

'She was only a baby then. But my grandmother could remember it. She used to talk to me about that time, when I was a kid. She's dead now.'

'Oh, I'm sorry.' Julie is silent a moment, then says cautiously, 'So — what was it like?'

Simon pauses as the Jeep bounces over a pothole. He and Julie are flung into the air, suspended for a second, then crash back into their seats. He says, 'My grandmother was pretty young, too, about our age, I guess, a new young wife. She remembered when the white men came. And the red-skinned men, too, that's what she called them, *man bilong nambis*, men from the coast. They were big and tall, they carried the *kago* for the white men, all the equipment, the supplies, tents and food and all the rest of it, a long line of men all laden down with boxes. They laughed at that, because carrying stuff was women's work . . .'

He glances across at her. 'It was a big shock, for everyone. The Europeans didn't know there was anyone living in the valleys. From the north coast, they could see mountains, and from the south coast, they could see mountains, and everyone had just always assumed it was the same mountain range. They had no idea there were huge wide valleys in between. So when they marched in and discovered there were a million people living here — it was quite a surprise.

'And of course, the Highlanders had no idea there was anyone living outside the valleys. Suddenly all these strangers arrive, aliens from another world. They didn't know what these men wanted, what they were doing here, on their tribe's land, in their territory. My grandmother said the women and children hid, the meris and pikininis, they were frightened.'

'It must have been like Martians landing,' says Julie.

Simon nods. 'Yeah, it must have seemed just like that ... They didn't know if these strangers were ghosts, or devils, or spirits from the lands of the sky. The strangers asked for food. But the men couldn't bring it to them, because that was women's work.' He catches Julie's eye, gives a wry grimace. 'But they soon realised the white men weren't spirits. They were men all right. The women found that out soon enough.'

Julie stares straight ahead, at the road. She can guess what the men must have wanted.

'The village men picked up whatever the strangers dropped, a tin lid, a matchbox, a cartridge case, any old rubbish that the white men threw away, and they'd wear it in their hair or in their beards, as if they were *kina* shells, precious shells — the shells were our money,' he adds. 'When Independence comes, the new currency is going to be called *kina* and *toea*, after those shells, did you know that?'

Julie shakes her head.

'Anyway, the whites had plenty of shells, they'd brought them up from the coast, and they gave them away in handfuls, scattered them around like they were worth nothing! And, of course, to the Europeans, they *were* worth nothing ... But everything was upside down, the rubbish the strangers threw away became really valuable, the shells were worth less because the white men had so many of them ...'

He glances sideways at Julie.

'My grandmother told me, in the beginning, they used to follow the men into the bush when they — relieved themselves. And afterwards, they used to pick up what they've left behind, wrap it in leaves, and take good care of it —'

'That's *disgusting*!' says Julie. '*Why?*'

'In case it had magic powers. Because they thought the white men might be devils or sorcerers. They didn't do that for long. Once they realised they were just ordinary men. Nothing to get excited about. That's what my grandmother said.' Simon veers to the edge of the road to avoid a truck coming the other way. 'Mind you, she was pleased when Mum moved in with my father. Share some of the wealth around. Help the wontoks.' He sees that she doesn't understand. '*Wontok*. One talk — people who speak the same language, the same *plestok*. Relatives, basically. You've got to help them out. If a wontok asks for help, you have to do it.' He falls silent. 'That's hard for Mum.'

'So does that mean they're your wontoks, too?'

'Yep.'

'So you have to help them out?'

'Yep.' A pause. 'But there are ways of doing it. Dad and Mum, they kind of figure it out together. They're a good team.'

Julie finds herself imagining what it must have been like for Dulcie's mother, or for Koki, when they were little girls like the ones she'd seen in the village this morning, but little girls who'd never seen a white person or dreamed that any world could exist outside the safe, enclosing wall of the mountains. Young girls, digging in the *kaukau* gardens, caring for babies, listening to the men boast about fighting, giggling with the other girls about their husbands or prospective husbands.

And then the lid was blown off the box.

Aeroplanes swooping overhead, dropping cargo like bombs. Airstrips and schools and churches springing up like fungus, the outside world flooding in; guns and money and food in tins; metal tools, metal weapons, instead of stone axes, spears and digging sticks; skirts and shirts and soap and books; cars and pills and razor blades, cameras and radios and movies and World War II.

Julie thinks of Koki, and of Dulcie, and their serene, peaceful faces. She thinks of all they've seen in their lifetimes, their universes turned not just upside down, as Simon says, but inside out.

'And what about your father, when he first arrived?' Julie says. 'What did he think of it all?'

Simon doesn't answer; for a moment, Julie thinks he hasn't heard. At last he says, 'Dad doesn't like talking about those pioneer days. He's talked about the war, a bit. But not the thirties, not first contact.'

'Why? It must have been so exciting — amazing to discover all those people —'

'He came to find gold,' says Simon. 'To make money. Not to expand the sum of human knowledge.'

'But still —'

'It wasn't pretty, you know,' says Simon. 'It was bloody dangerous. The locals thought they were being invaded. Well, they *were* being invaded. So they attacked. But there's not much a spear can do, or bows and arrows, against a rifle.'

Julie holds her breath. 'You mean — do you think Patrick might have —? He wouldn't have *shot* anyone, would he?'

Simon changes gear, his eyes fixed on the road. 'I found a box of stuff once. A journal, photographs, even some old films . . . They were under attack all the time, they had to defend themselves.'

'Who's *they*?' says Julie. 'Are you talking about the locals, or the explorers?'

Simon laughs, perplexed. 'Both, I guess — but I meant the Europeans. Sometimes they had to shoot first and ask questions later. Once the warriors knew what guns could do, they'd back off. It actually meant *less* bloodshed. If they shot just one man early on, and that scared the others into not fighting, they were actually *saving* lives, in the long run.' He glances at Julie. 'That makes sense, doesn't it?'

'Yes. No. I don't know. You think your father did that? Killed people?'

'I know he did. It's in his diaries.'

Julie stares out through the windscreen. A rainbow glows above the mountains; rain has polished the leaves and left behind glittering pools on the surface of the road. She tries to picture stiffly-moving old Patrick as a young man, raising a rifle to his shoulder, staring down a naked warrior who charges toward him, spear in hand, teeth bared. Does he shout a warning? The warrior doesn't, cannot, understand his peril. The rifle kicks; the warrior falls. There is blood on the ground; the women's mouths open in soundless screams. The picture is jerky, black and white, a scene from a silent film; it doesn't seem real.

They drive on in silence. Soon the buildings of the town appear on either side. They drive down the main street, past the post office with its forest of radio towers, and the two big trading stores — Carpenters and Burns Philp — the barefoot nationals wandering along the pavement. Julie can't help remembering Nadine's story about the woman who wore the sheet off the clothesline.

A couple of minutes later Simon pulls up the Jeep outside Tony's unit.

'Thanks for everything,' says Julie. 'For rescuing me, and lunch, and showing me Keriga, and everything.

Thanks for taking me to meet your parents . . . Not that it was like a *date*,' she adds hastily. 'I mean, I know it's not as if you were asking me to *marry* you or anything — not that that would be a bad thing — I mean —'

Her face is burning. She wonders if it's possible to actually die from mortification. She tugs at the door-handle and almost falls out of the Jeep.

'Just glad we got you home safely,' says Simon.

'Well, thanks!' calls Julie brightly, waving like an idiot.

The Jeep drives away, and she covers her face. Her cheeks are so hot with embarrassment she almost scorches her hands.

11

'On the nose with Barb, are we?' says Tony, after two nights of Julie's cooking.

Julie busies herself at the stove with the sausages. 'I think I upset her.'

'I heard about it.'

When Julie turns around, he is quietly smiling. 'Don't worry about it, mate,' he says. 'She'll come round.'

Julie pulls a face. 'You think so? She seems like the type to hold a grudge, to me.'

Tony laughs. 'You've got no problem with her son, though . . . You've made a friend for life there, by the looks of it.'

Julie brings the sausages to the table. 'Mm.'

Ryan has been at the house all day. He arrived on the doorstep bright and early, and settled in for a day of smooching on the couch. Which is nice enough, she supposes, but she doesn't want to spend her whole time in New Guinea locked inside the house with the curtains drawn, with Ryan's tongue in her mouth and his hands up her shirt. She tries to persuade him to walk with her to the library that Robyn has told her about, but he won't come. He sprawls on the couch and complains about how boring it is in Mt Hagen and how he can't wait to get back to Brisbane. 'Except for you,' he adds hastily. 'You're not boring.'

'Gee, thanks!' She lets him pull her down onto the couch, but after a few minutes she wriggles free and picks up Ryan's guitar. 'Play us a song?' she coaxes.

'What's the point?' he grumbles, but he takes the guitar and starts to strum, and soon he's absorbed in the music, his lank hair falling like a curtain across his face, and Julie, watching, thinks that perhaps she likes him best like this, when he's forgotten that she's there . . .

Tony polishes off his sausages. 'Not bad. Maybe we should ask Teddie and Spargo round one night.'

Julie looks up in alarm. 'I don't mind cooking for you, but I'm not ready for a dinner party.'

Tony laughs. 'Teddie won't be fit for a few days anyway. She's off sick. Hopefully it won't turn out to be dengue fever — Curry's a bit cranky, he's got no one to answer the phone for him now.'

The idea leaps from her mouth almost before it forms in her head. 'I could do that! I could help out. I've done typing at school. And I'd love to come in and see what you do, and how it all works.'

Tony's eyes brighten, but he says, 'You sure? Don't want to spoil your holiday . . . interfere with your social life, and all that . . .'

'It wouldn't,' Julie assures him.

'I'll have a word to Curry, then. It's not rocket science, just filing and that kind of thing. I reckon if Teddie can handle it, you should be able to do it standing on your head.'

Julie is surprised by the pride in his voice. She doesn't know where to look.

He says, rather wistfully, 'You've got your mother's brains. She was always too clever for me.'

Julie can't imagine Caroline and Tony together. Her mind baulks at the thought of it. They must have been different, when they were young; that's as far as her imagination will stretch. She jumps up and turns on the tap to fill the sink from the water tank. 'So, will you ring Curry now?'

*

Julie snaps awake in the morning when Tony's alarm shrills. She lies in bed, wondering if she's bitten off more than she can chew. Yes, she can answer a phone, and she's done three terms of typing at school. But what does she know about running an office, or an air charter business? Tony expects her to be clever; she imagines his disappointed face. *Never mind, mate, it doesn't matter* . . . She throws back the blanket. Her mouth is dry.

Tony has made her a coffee, strong and black, the way he likes it. Julie adds two spoonfuls of sugar, and a splash of UHT milk. She's almost used to the taste of it now, though she can't say she likes it. Nadine told her that when she's down south at school, she misses long-life milk. Julie wonders if, when she goes home, fresh milk will taste weird.

'Ready to go?'

She nods, still half-asleep, and follows him out to the car. Gibbo is just stumbling from his front door. Julie waves, and he blinks at her, baffled, as if he thinks he might be dreaming.

The sky is murky with night, the dawn just touching it, a dab of pale paint lowered into a glass of painting water. Or no — it's as if each touch of the brush removes some ink from the glass, the water growing cleaner, clearer, with every moment. The sky turns grey, then white. Julie leans her head back against the seat as the car hums along the road to the airport. Because the mountains screen the horizon, the world is quite light, she can see around her easily, before the sun itself rolls above the ranges and floods the valley with gold. Mist boils off the mountains like smoke.

'Best part of the day,' says Tony. 'Shame to waste it lying in bed.'

The HAC terminal is bustling. Pilots come in and out, sipping bitter coffee, grimacing, joshing one another, filling out forms, intently studying coloured pieces of paper. Later Julie will learn about flight plans and cargo manifests and NOTAMs, but for now it is all mysterious. Gibbo appears. 'Choose a job you love,' he says. 'And you'll never have to work a day in your life.'

'I know,' says Julie. 'You told me that already.'

In the cargo shed, the bois are busy shifting sacks of rice and coffee beans, heaving them onto the all-important big scales, while someone adjusts the brass weights along the slide and sings out the results. Allan Crabtree barks orders, his chest pigeon-puffed. When he sees Julie, he points to a chair. 'Sit there and stay out of the way. I'll get to you later.'

Of course, it will be Allan, not Tony, showing her what to do. She should have expected that. She hasn't thought this through.

But there is something intensely satisfying about being awake and part of all this busyness, while the rest of the world is asleep. The terminal hums like a machine. Before long, planes are being loaded. One by one, the pilots abandon their coffee mugs, drop their paperwork on the desk and stride out to start their engines. One by one, the planes roar into life, whirring like dragonflies with the early morning sun on their wings. In an orderly procession, they trundle onto the runway, then, at an invisible signal, they zoom along the tarmac, before lifting, as clumsy as beetles, as elegant as birds, into the soaring sky.

With a start, Julie realises that everyone has gone — everyone but her and Allan and the kago bois. Allan is barking at someone on the phone, and the bois are moving purposefully around in the shed, rearranging piles of boxes. The head boi, Joseph, pokes his head around the doorway to give her a friendly grin. Julie grins back, and feels better.

She collects up the coffee mugs and takes them out to the back kitchen to rinse and drain at the tiny sink, careful not to get in the workers' way. The whole building has a peculiar, particular smell — a mixture of condensed milk and cats, cleaning fluid and avgas — with the musty background New Guinea smell of sweat and smoke that she has almost stopped noticing. There is a box of kittens in one corner of the kitchen, to keep the mice down, she guesses, and the grubby table is littered with dog-eared playing cards, *Phantom* comics and well-thumbed copies of *Australasian Post*, with bosomy cover girls in skimpy bikini tops.

Allan marches in. 'Come on then, Miss McGinty, let's get cracking.'

To Julie's relief, he is much more amiable when there's no one around to yell at. The work he gives her isn't difficult, mostly answering the phone and taking messages, and typing out letters with messy sheets of carbon inserted between the pages, staining her fingertips purple. She tidies Teddie's desk and puts away some filing she'd pushed to one side. She feels competent and efficient and grown up.

All morning, the planes come and go. Some of the nearest airstrips are only ten minutes away. At lunchtime, Joseph produces a hot meal — roast meat, mashed potatoes, sweet corn, bread and butter — enough for everyone. The pilots stroll in, help themselves to coffee, and sprawl around the kitchen table with their ties unknotted. Julie is shy; she carries her lunch into the office and eats at her desk.

When it's safe to come out, she takes her plate back to the kitchen, and kneels by the kitten box. She lifts out one tiny scrap of fur and rubs it against her cheek.

Joseph comes in and squats beside her. He croons softly as his calloused, scarred finger gently reaches into the box and scratches a kitten's fur.

'*Dispela*, I take home,' he says. '*Long pikinini*.'

'You have children, Joseph? How many?'

He grins. '*Faipela*.'

'Five! Boys or girls?'

'*Tripela gel, tupela boi*.'

They chat brokenly about his children for a few minutes, but Julie is hardly listening. Joseph is a father, a grown man, and yet every day of his working life, he is called *boi* by men young enough to be his sons. Shame spreads warmly through her. She resolves at that moment never again to call an adult national a *boi*. He is a person; not just part of the exotic scenery.

By now it's afternoon, and the planes are coming back, dropping gently from the sky onto the runway and nosing their way back to the terminal, like tired horses snuffling back to their stable.

The morning's flurry is repeated in reverse — the planes unloaded, the passengers disgorged, the cargo stacked for collection. The pilots lounge at the front counter, or prop their feet on the kitchen table. More paperwork piles up in the tray on Julie's desk. The day has raced by.

'How did she go?' asks Tony.

'Not bad,' says Allan. 'Not bad at all.'

That night Ryan rings to complain about how boring his day has been. 'Thank God I can come round to your place tomorrow.'

'Well — your dad wants me to work again. I said I would.'

'Jeez, how much are you getting paid for this?'

Julie is embarrassed to admit that she hasn't even asked about money. She's not entirely sure that she'll be paid at all. 'Plenty!' she says, resolving to ask Allan first thing tomorrow.

'So you should be. It's ruining the whole holiday.'

'I think it's kind of fun.' And it is; it's like playing offices when she was little, except that the typewriter and the telephone, with its sophisticated three separate lines, the cashbox and the filing cabinets, the notice-board with its flight roster, are all real. She feels deft and cool, rolling the paper into the typewriter and making the keys clatter with a din that fills the room.

By the next day, she has already become part of the tribe. 'Morning, Julie.' 'G'day, Julie.' 'Jeez, you're bloody keen, up at this hour. Don't let the old man work you too hard.'

Julie and Allan work well together. 'Makes a nice change, bit of peace and quiet, none of that bloody racket Teddie Spargo blasts through the place,' he growls.

It hasn't even occurred to Julie to switch the radio on.

'Bloody hell,' he says later. 'Can't remember the last time I saw the top of that desk. I'd forgotten what colour it was.'

'I just thought I'd tidy up a bit —'

As she types, she imagines herself living here, working every day, getting up with the sunrise. She could leave school; she is old enough. She could live with Tony all year round . . . There is no reason why she couldn't do it. She could stay here forever. Teddie will have a baby soon, everyone says so. Allan will need someone in the office. Her fingers fly across the keys, her mind busy with daydreams.

In reality, if she ended up working as a mere secretary she knows her mother would have fifty kinds of fit. All those Women's Lib, you-can-do-anything lectures wasted . . .

And if Julie did stay here, she would miss her mum. It was funny, they were getting on much better now that they were hundreds of miles apart. Caroline's letters from Sydney were funny and affectionate, sprinkled with more hugs and kisses than she ever gives Julie in real life. And it is much harder to have arguments in cramped airletters than face to face. Her mother had actually rung her a couple of nights ago, a quick, cheerful phone call, and before Caroline hung up, she'd actually said, *I love you* . . .

If Julie stayed in New Guinea, she would miss Rachel, too, and her other friends. Maybe Rachel would come and visit in the holidays. Julie could show her everything . . .

That afternoon, Allan calls her aside and gives her an envelope with twenty dollars inside. It's the first money she has ever earned in a real workplace. She clutches it against her chest.

Allan eyes her reflectively. 'Shame you're not a couple of years older, Miss McGinty. I'd offer you the job.'

Her first reaction is a rush of pleasure: perhaps her dream really could come true. But what she actually says, before she can stop herself, is, 'Barbara might not like that.'

Allan scowls. 'Barb's not the bloody boss here!'

'Yes, Mr Crabtree,' says Julie meekly.

He softens. 'Don't you worry about Barb. Nadine told me the whole story about Koki. You did the right thing.'

Julie gazes modestly at the desk, hoping he'll say more, but at that moment his eye is caught by a movement outside, in the waiting area. He shoots out of the office like a pea from a blowpipe.

'What the hell are you doing here?'

There is a breathless, mumbled reply; a mumble that Julie recognises. She hurries out behind the counter and sees Ryan, dusty and bedraggled, pushing the damp hair off his flushed and sweaty face.

'Just rode out to say hi,' he mutters. Julie can see his bike, dropped on the gravel outside. He shoots her an agonised glance from beneath his fringe.

'You didn't ride ten kays out from town for the pleasure of saying hi to me!' barks Allan. 'Your girlfriend's busy! We've got four flights due to land in the next half hour, and Julie's got better things to do than waste time canoodling with you!'

'Jeez, give me a break!' says Ryan.

'I haven't got time to deal with you now. You can make yourself useful, or you can piss off.'

Ryan eyes him warily. 'What do you mean, make myself useful?'

'Joseph'll find you a job. You could sweep out the shed. The wall out front could do with a coat of paint. That bathroom's a disgrace, someone needs to clean that bloody toilet.'

'I'm not doing that!' Ryan's face is pink, with indignation now, rather than exertion. 'That's a boi's job!'

'It's bloody work, that's what you're afraid of!' roars Allan, his own face purple. 'Jesus Christ, who would have thought I'd raise a son who's scared of a bit of hard work? I started off in the cane fields at Bundaberg! Now that was bloody hard work! You wouldn't know hard work if it jumped up and bit you on the arse!'

'A plane's coming in, Curry,' says Julie.

Through the big window, a blue-and-white plane sways slightly as it lowers itself toward the ground, the sun glinting off its windshield.

'Right!' yells Allan. He swings on his heel and stalks off through the doorway to the cargo shed. 'Joseph!'

Julie turns to Ryan, thinking he might be grateful to be rescued, but he's already pushed through the glass doors and picked up his fallen bike from the gravel. As Julie watches, he swings his leg over the saddle and pedals away.

12

'Curry's got a new client, he's shouting us all drinks at the Highlander,' says Tony over the phone, his voice a shade too loud. In the background, Julie can hear the clink of glasses and the muted roar of the bar. 'You'll be right, won't you? Why don't you pop over to the Crabtrees' before it gets dark? Barb'll run you home later.'

'Mm.' Julie curls the phone cord round her finger.

'You and Barb are mates again, aren't you?'

'Sort of. Yeah, I might do that. See you.'

'I shouldn't be too late,' he says. 'Gotta work tomorrow.'

After she hangs up, Julie decides that an evening to herself is just what she needs. She eats the spaghetti she'd prepared before Tony rang, and two helpings of ice cream. She'd quite like to speak to her mother, but Julie feels shy about ringing up someone she's never met, Caroline's Sydney friend; and it's only a few days since Caroline last rang, anyway.

Julie slots a cassette into the tape player and turns up the volume while she indulges in a long, hot bath.

She could write some letters — she owes one to her mother, and she hasn't written to her friend Rachel for a fortnight. But Rachel and Caroline seem very far away, and letters are more fun to receive than they are to write . . . Without consciously deciding to do it, Julie finds the telephone under her ear, and her finger dialling the number for Keriga. Perhaps enough time has passed for Simon to forget the humiliation of their last conversation. She decides, if Patrick or Dulcie answers, she'll pretend it's a wrong number.

But it's Simon.

'Hi . . . It's Julie. I'm not interrupting anything, am I?'

'No, it's okay. I was just reading to Dad.'

'Reading out loud?'

'His eyes get tired these days. He loves Graham Greene.'

Julie hasn't read any Graham Greene. She makes a noncommittal noise.

Simon says, 'Don't get me wrong, I'd prefer a spy novel. There's a new John le Carre out; it's meant to be really good, but I haven't read it yet . . . Graham Greene's a bit sad for me.'

'So the spy stories are happy, are they?'

Simon laughs. 'Fair point.'

Julie doesn't want to tell him that she hasn't even heard of John le Carre.

'So,' says Simon after a moment. 'How's your boy-friend?'

Julie's heart leaps into her throat. 'Do you mean Ryan?'

'What, is there another one?'

'No! But . . . Ryan's not really my boyfriend.'

'Not really?'

'Well, he's not,' says Julie. There is a pause, then she admits, 'But *he* might think he is.'

'That's unfortunate,' says Simon.

For Ryan? Or for him? Julie says, 'It is a bit awkward.'

'So, are you planning to break the bad news?'

'I thought he might just . . . get the hint. Eventually.'

'You should put the poor guy out of his misery.'

'I'm only here for a few more weeks. Then I'm going back to Melbourne and he'll be in Brisbane.'

'But what about when you come back?'

A pause. 'I hadn't thought of that.'

'You might get lucky, his family might *go finis*. Then you'll never need to see him again.'

'I mean, I hadn't thought that I might come back.'

The wild daydream about leaving school and working at HAC is one thing. The idea of coming back, year after year, the way the Crabtree kids do, is something else: a solid possibility, something real. Now that she's facing it head on, the thought of leaving New Guinea and never coming back blows a desolate chill through Julie. She isn't sure that she can talk about it. She clears her throat. 'Your dad never even tried to leave, did he?'

'No, never. Even when his parents died, he didn't go back for the funerals. He didn't get on with his family. I've never met any of them. Dad says he made his own family here.' Simon's voice is sombre. 'He says the only thing he's ever missed is the sea.'

Julie tucks her feet beneath her. 'You're so lucky, knowing exactly what you're going to do, working at Keriga.'

'I've been wondering if I ought to have a crack at politics, one day.' There is a pause. 'I've never told anyone that before.'

'Wow,' says Julie. 'That would be amazing.'

'Well, I don't know. I don't know if I'm cut out for all that arguing. Maybe what this country needs most is good businessmen, maybe I should just concentrate on that.'

'There's plenty of time. I mean, if you were going to become prime minister, it wouldn't be for years and years . . .'

'That's true. What about you, anyway? What are your plans?'

'I don't really know what I'm going to do,' says Julie. For a moment she considers confiding her running-away-from-school plan, but what if he scoffs at her, or tells her it's impossible?

'There's plenty to do,' says Simon. 'Up here. A whole new nation, starting out. We can make it anything we want. If you wanted to come back — there's medicine, teaching, journalism —'

'I worked in the office at HAC. I quite liked that.'

'You could be a public servant. When I'm in parliament, you can come and work for me!'

'Hey, why couldn't I get elected?' says Julie. '*I'll* be in parliament, and you can come and work for *me*.'

'You'll need to become a citizen first.'

'Okay, I will . . . Maybe I could learn to fly! I'll come up here and be a pilot like Tony.' Excitement rises in her. She doesn't have to just sit in the office; she can fly the planes! There are loads of things she could do! For the first time, rather than looming like a black hole, the future sparks with possibility. Maybe not actually flying, though; she's still a little too nervous for that.

They've been talking for almost two hours when the power goes out and cuts off the phone. Blinking in the sudden darkness, Julie hangs up. Tony hasn't come home. So much for *shouldn't be too late*. Suddenly she feels cross and abandoned. She quite likes the way Tony treats her as an adult, but that doesn't mean he can leave her here alone while he stays out all night.

She gropes her way around in the darkness, trying to remember which switches were flicked on, and turning them off, and feels proud of herself for thinking to switch on the porch light for Tony, in case the power is restored before he arrives home. It's not worth digging out the candles. She brushes her teeth in the dark, and goes to bed.

*

Julie wakes to a blaze of light in her face. She screws up her eyes against the light, thinking confusedly that she's forgotten to turn off a switch, and the power has come back on. She blinks and focuses.

But it's the beam of a torch shining in her face. And behind the torch, the dim shape of a man.

She has a split second of absolute clarity. It's a burglar. He is in the flat, with her. And she forgot to check that the back door was bolted before she went to bed.

The torch beam plays across her face. Then, unhurried, the dark figure turns away. The spotlight of the torch dips and swings over the walls of her bedroom, sweeping across Holly Hobbie, and Julie catches a glimpse of the man's face. Casually, he turns and strolls through the doorway.

It's his nonchalance that strikes a shaft of white-hot anger through her. He couldn't care less that she's woken up and seen him; he isn't scared of her at all! Without thinking, she snatches up the only weapon within reach — the hardback novel on her bedside table — and hurls it at his back. She misses; he is already out of the room.

'Get out! Get out!' Julie leaps from the bed and grabs the chair with both hands, by the leg and the back, and brandishes it. Swear words pour from her lips, as fluent and furious as Curry Crabtree himself. Screaming abuse, Julie throws herself after the intruder, and as she comes into the living room, she sees him run. He lopes toward the open back door (she knew it) and she chases him out into the backyard.

'Piss off! *Raus!* Get out of our house!' she screams, incoherent with rage.

A grumble of dry thunder rolls around the horizon, and by a flicker of lightning she sees him scramble over the sagging back fence, a dark shape, clumsy as a bear.

'And stay out!' she yells. Her hands are shaking as she lowers the chair.

Then Gibbo is running across the grass, faster than she's ever seen him move. 'Jesus wept! You all right, Julie?'

Tony races up behind them. 'What happened? Bloody hell!' He throws his arms around her. His breath is warm and beery.

Julie leans into the hug. 'I'm fine, I'm fine.' Dimly, as if through thick morning mist, she processes the sounds

141

she'd heard a moment before: the crunch of gravel as the car pulled up, the sweep of headlights at the front of the unit. Maybe that was what had made him run, not her chasing him at all — or maybe it was Gibbo running outside —

Gibbo says, 'You sure you're all right? He didn't — you know — touch you?'

Mutely Julie shakes her head. She feels Tony flinch. He puts his arm around her shoulders.

'Thanks, mate, I'll take it from here.'

'Okay.' Gibbo shrugs, and retreats to his own unit, throwing worried looks over his shoulder.

Tony leads Julie inside and sits her down at the table while he bolts the front and back doors, and checks all the windows.

'I left the back door unlocked,' she says.

He shakes his head. 'You just can't do that, love. You have to —'

The white-hot anger flares again. 'It's not my fault! You should have been here! You said you wouldn't be late!' She spreads her hands flat on the tabletop. 'What if he'd attacked me? What if —'

'I know, I know! Shit, I'm sorry!' Tony drops into a chair. More quietly he says, 'I thought you could take care of yourself.'

Julie says, 'I'm only sixteen.'

'I'm sorry.' Tony runs his hand over his head. He says, 'I'm no good at this. This dad stuff.'

Julie stares at the table. Thunder growls around the valley. The power is back on.

'Hot drink,' says Tony. 'That's what we need.'

Slowly he stands and makes his way to the sink to fill the electric jug. His face is grey beneath its stubble, and the hair that fringes his bald pate is all fluffed up like a frightened bird. He makes two steaming mugs of Milo and pushes one across the table to Julie. He says again, 'I'm so sorry, love.'

Julie looks up. 'I should have locked the door. It was my fault.'

Tony shakes his head. 'And I should have been here.'

They sip at their Milo without speaking for a few moments.

Julie sighs and looks around. 'I think he got the radio. And my purse is gone.'

'The beer from the fridge. And that frozen chook.'

Their eyes meet and they give a weak laugh at the idea of a burglar who'd stoop to stealing a frozen chicken.

'Poor bugger,' says Tony. 'Almost feel sorry for him.' He flattens his hair with his hand and blows out a gusty breath. 'Do you think we could put off ringing your mum until morning?'

Julie stares at him blankly. 'Why do you want to ring *her*?'

'You've had a fright — don't you want to talk to your mum? Anyway,' his voice sinks so low she can hardly hear it, 'you'll want to go home now, won't you?'

'No! Of course not! And I didn't really have a fright. I wasn't frightened. Not while it was happening.' This is true, she realises. Chasing the burglar, whirling the chair in the air, she'd felt more excited than scared. Even now, her heart is banging in her chest and adrenalin races through her veins. She says, 'I was just — *angry*. I *chased* him. I wanted to *hit* him.'

Tony shakes his head. 'You want to be careful, love. That's how I got this.' He runs the tip of his finger down the channel of his scar. 'That was from an axe. Because I lost my temper.' He looks at her. 'Next time, Julie, promise me — don't do anything silly. Though touch wood, there won't be a next time . . .' He raps on the tabletop.

'Okay,' she says. 'If you promise me you won't tell Caroline about tonight.'

Reluctantly he smiles. 'Deal.'

'I don't want to go home.' She sighs out a long breath. 'It's like — everything is more *alive* here. I feel more alive here.'

'Must be all the electricity in the air.'

Right on cue, lightning splits the sky outside like the flick of a whip.

'And the way the light looks, after it rains,' she says. 'It's so — *intense*.'

He laughs at her earnestness. 'Yeah,' he agrees. 'Sometimes I feel as if I lost a layer of skin when I moved up here.' He takes a gulp of Milo. 'Beautiful people, too.' He gazes into space for a moment, then rouses himself. 'You shouldn't let that idiot tonight spoil it for you.'

'I won't.' Julie wraps her hands around the mug. 'Do you ever think about going home?'

'Down south, you mean? That's the thing, isn't it? I reckon this is home now.' He looks into his Milo. 'Gets a bit lonely sometimes. I can't deny that. But I wouldn't want to leave.'

'What if the Crabtrees *go finis*?'

He shrugs. 'I'll get another job. They'll always need pilots in the Highlands. I wouldn't want to work anywhere else, that's the truth.'

'What about Independence?' Julie hesitates. 'It's so confusing. Simon Murphy can't wait; he's so excited about it. But everyone else says there'll be riots in the streets and everything will fall apart.'

'I dunno, love. The people will be the same. And the electricity in the air. And the light, after it rains.'

Julie reaches out to squeeze his hand. Tony looks startled, but after a second he gives an awkward squeeze in return. She says shyly, 'Do you think I could come back? Could I visit you again?'

His face lights up. 'Of course you can!' Then his eyes drop. 'If you want to. I don't expect you to make any promises. You're getting older, you'll be busy with your own life soon, boyfriends and study and work and all that. I don't expect you to keep running up here to see your old man, at the arse end of nowhere.'

Julie laughs. 'I thought we just agreed it was the best place in the world.'

'Yeah, I think we did.'

'Anyway, I don't know what I'm going to do. I might come back and work here — be a teacher, or — work in an office or something . . .' She doesn't quite dare yet to bring up the possibility of giving up school and staying on here; she'll work up to that gradually. Or perhaps she already knows, deep down, that it will only ever be a daydream. She says in a rush, 'You're so lucky, that you've found the place where you belong.'

'They say once this place gets into your blood it never lets you go. Like a fishhook in your heart. It keeps tugging away at you, like it or not.' He smiles shyly. 'I had an idea the other day. I was thinking we could take a little trip, a weekend away, after Christmas, you and me and the Crabtrees? A weekend in Wewak, up on the coast. It's bloody beautiful; you ought to see it, like bloody Paradise. You could call it a Christmas present if you like. I didn't know what else to get you. What do you reckon?'

'Oh, Tony, thank you!' Julie flings her arms around his neck and kisses his shiny red cheek. 'I'd *love* it!'

It flashes through her mind that she could say, *I don't need to ring my mum when I've got my dad here*. But she's too shy to actually say it aloud.

Later, lying in bed, wriggling her toes between cool sheets, adrenalin still coursing through her blood, she has a brilliant idea. She'll invite the Murphys to come to Wewak too, Simon and Patrick and Dulcie — so that Patrick can see the sea. She'll ask Tony in the morning.

Julie rolls over and cuddles the blanket under her chin. She marvels at herself. She never knew she had such courage in her: to stare down an intruder, to actually chase him out of the house! Caroline would never believe it . . .

And then a cold trickle of shame runs down her spine. Brave enough to face a burglar, but not brave enough to break up with Ryan. Why hadn't she rung Ryan tonight when she wanted someone to talk to? Wasn't that what girls with boyfriends were supposed to do?

It isn't that she doesn't like him; maybe she just doesn't like him *enough* . . .

She thrusts that thought aside. For now, she wants to feel proud of herself, and she won't let Ryan spoil that, not tonight.

13

In the week before Christmas there is a film night, a fundraiser for the Lions Club. Nadine tells Julie that the arrival of a new film is always a cause for excitement. 'But then everyone gets hold of it, the Lions, the golf club, somebody's birthday party, the fleapit — that's the cinema. One year I saw *Cat Ballou* five times.'

Julie has been to the cinema, where the expats sit upstairs in the gallery, in padded seats, while the nationals sit on rough wooden benches down below. She says uncomfortably, 'So what film is on tonight?'

Nadine shrugs. 'I dunno, but it's newish. Science fiction, I think.'

The Crabtrees offer to take Julie with them, but she goes back to the unit to wait for Tony. The rain is roaring down, drumming so loudly on the tin roof that she can hardly hear the telephone when it rings.

'Julie, it's Allan. Just wanted to let you know, it looks like Tony might be a bit late back.'

149

She jams her finger in her ear to mute the noise of the rain. 'Do you mean he's not back yet? He didn't get in before the rain started?'

'Nothing to worry about. It's not that unusual, getting rained in. He's probably stuck on the airstrip at Koinambe.'

'So — will he be back tonight, or not?'

'He might be marooned overnight, he might have to spend the night in the plane and fly back in the morning. Depends on the weather. Look, it happens from time to time. I'll bet he comes swanning in first thing tomorrow, howling for a coffee and a plate of bacon and eggs.'

'Okay,' she says in a small voice. After the burglary, the prospect of spending a night alone in the unit is not hugely appealing.

'Tell you what,' says Allan, his voice faint and distant. 'You're going to the Lions' movie night, aren't you? I'll get Andy and Teddie to take you along. Then if Tony does turn up, he can take you home. Okay?'

'You think he might still turn up then?' she says hopefully.

'N-ah. Not while it's pissing down like this. And if he does, by God, I'll give him a bollocking he won't forget in a hurry.'

About half an hour later, Teddie arrives on the doorstep, gasping and half-drowned, her hair plastered to her head. 'Look at my umbrella, totally useless! I might as well have put a hanky over my head ...'

She comes inside, dripping all over the floor. 'Have you got water coming in? Andy and me had to put towels under our door; it was *flooding* in. I think our gutters must be blocked ... You really know you're in the tropics on a day like this! Got your overnight bag? Curry says you may as well stay the night with us, if Tony doesn't make it. Andy had to sleep in the plane once, at Mendi, he said it was the longest night of his life. He was fine, though. Just uncomfortable ... And at least he was dry. Dryer than we are, probably. Tony must have a raincoat somewhere ...'

She wanders into Tony's room, where Julie has never dared to enter, and emerges with a huge cracked old Driza-Bone. It's like draping herself in a pterodactyl's wing. Julie locks up carefully, clutching her overnight bag, and follows Teddie out into the deluge.

'Will they call off the film night if it keeps raining like this?' Julie yells, as they slip and slide up the street to the Spargos' house. Water pours in rivers along the ditches by the side of the road.

'Oh, no. A little drop of rain won't put anyone off.'

She smiles at Julie, blinking the water out of her eyes, then reaches out to grab her hand, and they swing their hands and shriek as they run through the rain.

They eat a cheerful, improvised meal of grilled cheese on toast, then the three of them pile into Andy's car. The rain has eased off slightly, and Julie begins to feel more hopeful that Tony might actually make it back tonight after all. It isn't dark yet, and how far away is Koinambe anyway? If it's a half-hour flight, he could easily sneak in before sunset. Andy and Teddie have made up a bed for her on the floor of their spare room, with a sleeping bag and a thin foam mattress, but Julie would prefer her own bed, with Tony's snores reverberating through the thin wall, the now-familiar shadows playing on the ceiling, and the croak of frogs in the water tank. Andy seems convinced that Tony will be spending the night in his plane; he tells Julie how, when he did it, he made himself a nest from rice sacks and bolts of cloth and slept quite snugly.

'That's not what you told me,' says Teddie.

'Well, of course I told you I'd rather have been at home in bed with you.' Andy winks at Julie over his shoulder. 'We'd only been married for a month. *Now* I'd appreciate not getting kicked in the ribs all night — ow!'

Teddie has slapped him on the arm.

When they arrive at the crowded wooden hall that the Lions are borrowing for the night, Julie looks around for Simon Murphy. But although the entire white population of Mt Hagen seems to have turned out for the occasion, she can't see him or Patrick anywhere. Julie supposes this is one of those events that the Murphys are not invited to. Robyn Johansson gives her a cheery wave from the other side of the hall, and Julie waves back.

Andy fetches beers for himself and Teddie; he offers one to Julie, but she says no. Ryan, Nadine and Barbara are on the other side of the hall, securing places near the front among the rows of folding seats. There is no sign of Allan. Julie sees Ryan gaze around at the crowd, and instinctively she steps back behind the shelter of Andy's shoulder. She can't sit near the front anyway, she argues to herself; if Tony comes in late, he'll never be able to find her all the way down there. She makes sure she sits at the end of a row, just in case. Feeling slightly guilty, she promises herself she'll go and find Ryan after the film. It's just that, tonight, she feels like concentrating on the movie, without worrying about how far Ryan's hand is travelling up her thigh . . .

The film does turn out to be science fiction, as Nadine predicted, a recent movie called *Soylent Green*, which Julie hasn't seen. It's set in an overcrowded future where food is running out, and people rely on a plankton-based wafer for sustenance. Julie watches the hero running back and forth across the screen. The hum of rain on the roof, which drowned out some of the early dialogue, gradually peters out. She wonders how Tony is getting on, shut inside his plane. She hopes it's an Islander, with more leg room than the Baron. If he's lucky, he might have some food on board, some chocolate maybe, something more palatable than tins of fish or raw rice. At least he won't have to turn to Soylent Green . . .

A touch on her shoulder makes her jump. Allan Crabtree is squatting beside her; in the flickering light from the projector, he motions with his head for her to follow him out of the hall. Julie stumbles after him, her heart thudding, as if her body knows more than her mind is prepared to acknowledge. She tells herself that perhaps Allan is going to suggest that she stay the night with the Crabtrees, in a proper bed in Nadine's room, instead of the Spargos' camping mattress.

Outside, the clouds have cleared. The moon is almost full, and the sky is blazing with stars.

'Julie,' says Allan. 'I've got some bad news, love.'

He's found out that Tony is not stuck on the airfield at Koinambe. His plane had definitely taken off through the Kumil Gap, heading for Hagen. He didn't turn back, and he has not arrived, and as far as they could tell, he hasn't touched down anywhere else on the way. His plane is missing.

'I'm so sorry, love. But we have to assume — with weather like we had today — there's a good chance he's gone down.'

Teddie and Andy have come out after them. They are standing close to Julie, warm shadowy presences in the dark. Teddie lets out a hiccupping gasp. Andy's low voice says, 'Oh, no. No, I don't believe it.'

Julie is numb. She can't gasp; she can't speak. She hears Teddie and Andy talking, their words muffled, as if her head is underwater.

Teddie says, 'He — he might be all right, though? Even if —?'

'The country round there is pretty rough,' says Allan. 'We won't know for sure for a day or two. But I wouldn't — well, we shouldn't get our hopes up.'

Andy swears. 'I don't get it! Tony's so careful. He never takes risks. No see; no go. He hammered that into me for months.'

Teddie covers her face with her hands. Allan lays his hand heavily on Julie's shoulder, and his beefy fingers squeeze her collarbone so hard it seems he might snap it like a wishbone.

And Julie remembers then that they all know Tony so much better than she does. She's only been here for a few weeks; they've lived with him, worked beside him, been his friend for months and years. They have more right to be upset than she does. She wraps her arms around herself and shivers. Again, as she did at Teddie and Andy's party, she has that feeling of watching herself, of being an impostor.

'You all right, love?' says Allan.

Julie nods.

Allan looks at Andy. 'Better take her home. You got anything to help her sleep?'

'Yes,' says Teddie. 'I've got something.'

'If not, I'll get something from Gibbo,' says Andy.

They bundle her into the car. The ride back into town is a nightmare jumble of sinister shadows, trees that flare suddenly in the headlights then seem to jerk away, the red eyes of the road markers glaring out of the darkness.

She hears Teddie say in a low voice, 'He must have been rushing back for Julie. After the break-in —'

'Shut up!' says Andy sharply, and shoots a look at Julie in the rear-view mirror.

But their words don't sink in, they glance off her like raindrops off glass.

Andy and Teddie are kind and gentle. Teddie helps her to undress, and gives her a pill to swallow. She hugs her, and tells her not to give up hope. Andy warms some milk in a saucepan, to wash down the pill, but he accidentally lets it boil over on the stove, and the stink of burnt milk floods through the whole house.

After this night, for the rest of her life, the smell of burning milk will make Julie retch. Sometimes it will take her a moment to remember why, but it's her body, holding grimly onto knowledge that her mind has tried to forget.

14

After that first night, Barbara takes over. She marches into Teddie and Andy's house early the next morning and hustles Julie into the car.

'You'd better stay with us for now,' she says briskly. 'There's a spare bed in Nadine's room; you can bunk in with her.'

Julie puts up a feeble struggle. 'I'd like to go home.' She means, *to Tony's place*.

Barbara pats her knee. 'Of course you do. As soon as we can manage it. We're having a bit of trouble tracking down your mother. Perhaps she's gone away? Have you heard from her?'

'She's in Sydney, staying with a friend. I've got the number somewhere.'

Barbara nods. 'We'll find her, don't you worry.'

Christmas is only two days away. Julie leans her head against the cold glass of the window. The car smells of dog. She thinks of the gifts she'd carefully wrapped for Tony and hidden under her bed. A lump rises into her throat. She closes her eyes and swallows hard.

*

Barbara spends most of the day holding the phone to her ear with her shoulder while she scribbles on a notepad. There's no answer from Caroline's friend's number.

'Perhaps they've gone away?' Barbara looks at Julie. 'Did your mother mention anything like that?'

'I haven't spoken to her for a little while . . .'

'Hm.'

Clearly Barbara thinks this is odd, even reprehensible, but she is kind enough not to say so. She leaves messages for Caroline everywhere. Even the police have been notified; although, as Barbara says in exasperation, they're being no help at all.

Julie sits numbly on the couch with Ryan's arm around her, while Nadine tries to distract her with her pets. Julie leans against the warmth of Ryan and the circle of his arms feels like safety. He doesn't speak. He doesn't say, *I'm so sorry*, or *poor Tony, I can't believe it*; he just holds her. Sometimes she lets Nadine nurse her hand, as if it's one of her wounded animals, and Koki brings cups of sweet tea and rubs her back with her callused hand. Roxy the dog licks anxiously at her ankles and whines softly, as if she knows what's wrong. Everyone is kind, but Julie knows she can't start to cry, because once she starts, she won't be able to stop. She leans against Ryan, and concentrates on not letting herself cry.

She wishes she was at home — home in Melbourne. She could be hanging out with Rachel, eating doughnuts at Southland, skating at Rollerama. She wishes she could lose herself watching TV. Her head feels full of cold fog.

Allan comes in and shakes his head. He murmurs gruffly to Barbara, but Julie overhears. They've found the plane. It's in the Jimi Valley, not far from Koinambe. But it will take days to reach the wreckage and retrieve Tony's body. There's no mistake; there will be no miracle, no reprieve. But somehow she still can't feel it.

In the afternoon, she goes to bed, takes another of Teddie's pills, and sleeps like a felled tree. She wakes in the middle of the night and hears Nadine's snuffly breathing in the next bed, and for a second she doesn't know where she is.

Tony's dead. It slices down like a guillotine blade. She turns her face into the pillow and the tears flood out of her. She sobs, choking into the pillow, so she won't wake Nadine. She thinks about creeping across the hallway to Ryan's room, sliding into his bed, for the comfort of his eager body, for the oblivion; she almost does it; it's only exhaustion that pulls her under and keeps her paralysed, tangled in the blankets like an animal in the net.

*

On Christmas morning, she wakes up late. Nadine's bed is empty. Julie lies unmoving beneath the blankets for as long as she can bear it; she dreads dragging her grief into the Crabtrees' family Christmas. But at last the hollow, lonely feeling overwhelms her. She pulls on some clothes and shuffles out into the big living room where the lopsided Christmas tree fills the air with the scent of pine.

But it's only Nadine who sits beneath the tree with Christmas wrappings strewn around her. The others sit motionless, looking as shell-shocked as Julie feels. The radio is on, but it's not wafting the expected Christmas carols; a newsreader is speaking. Ryan beckons Julie over and she wedges herself into the armchair beside him.

'The news once again: Cyclone Tracy has devastated the city of Darwin. The extent of damage is unknown at this stage, but early reports indicate —'

Julie leans forward and holds her head in her hands. It seems like some kind of grotesque joke. For a wild second, she wonders if Caroline has gone to Darwin; if her mother has been killed; if she's an orphan now. The next instant she realises how unlikely this is.

But over the next few days, photographs appear in the newspapers: flattened buildings, piles of rubble, uprooted trees, mile after mile of torn and twisted sheets of tin and fibro, scattered at random where a town had once stood. And it's as if nature has echoed the chaos in her own heart.

*

On Christmas night, Caroline rings.

'Oh, God, darling,' she says. 'I'm so sorry. I can't believe it. Trust Tony to wait until you were there to fly himself into a mountain. Oh dear, poor Tony. I didn't mean that . . . Julie? Are you there?'

'Yes.'

'Are you all right? You're not on your own, are you? There's someone looking after you? These Crabtree people?'

'Yes.'

'Well, tell them it's only for another couple of days. As soon as I can get your flight changed, you'll be on your way home. Oh, dear. If only it wasn't Christmas — it's impossible to get anyone to answer the phone. I wonder if it might not be easier from your end? Perhaps I should talk to this — Belinda, is it?'

'Barbara.'

'Yes, Barbara, put her on, will you, darling? I think I'd better speak to her.'

Julie's hand tightens around the receiver. 'No.'

'Sorry, darling, what was that?'

Julie says, more loudly, 'No!'

'What? What's the matter?'

'I don't want to come back yet. I want to wait —'
She swallows. 'They haven't even found his body yet.
I want to stay until the funeral.'

'Oh. Well, I suppose — When do you think that's
likely to be?'

'I don't know.'

'Sorry, darling, I couldn't hear you —'

'I don't know!'

A pause. Julie can imagine her mother, harassed,
pushing her hair back from her forehead. 'Sweetheart,
you can't just impose on these Crabtree people indefi-
nitely. What are we talking about? Days, weeks?'

'I don't know. They don't mind me being here. Allan
said I could stay as long as I liked.'

'Yes, well, of course he *said* that.' Another pause.
'Who is organising the funeral, anyway?'

'I don't know; Allan, I suppose.'

'That's his manager, isn't it?'

'They were friends, Mum.'

'Perhaps I should come up there myself,' says Caroline.
'Maybe that's the best idea. We can't leave it all to
strangers.'

'You don't have to do that! People up here look after each other; Tony had plenty of friends. There's no need to —'

But Caroline speaks over her. 'That's the pips, darling. Love you, goodbye —'

'Bye,' says Julie. But the line is dead.

*

'Oh, hell,' says Barbara suddenly on Boxing Day. 'The Wewak trip. We were supposed to leave on Saturday. I'll have to phone up and cancel the hotel.'

Julie looks up. 'Do we have to cancel?'

'As far as I know, it's all paid for,' says Allan. 'But there shouldn't be any problem getting a refund. Under the circumstances.'

The lump in Julie's throat is so hard she can barely force out the words. 'I don't want to cancel it. Tony said it was my Christmas present.'

Barbara shoots a quick glance at Allan. 'But, Julie, surely you don't feel like a holiday at the beach? Just a few days after your father —?'

Julie's throat is tight. She mutters, 'I really want to go.'

'Ah, to hell with it,' growls Allan. 'Why not? Where's the bloody harm?'

Barbara draws him aside. She murmurs, 'It looks heartless. Even you can see that. Anyway, she might have gone home by then. As soon as Caroline can organise her visa —'

'Mac wanted her to see Wewak,' says Allan loudly. 'Why the hell shouldn't she go? What's the point of cancelling? It was the last bloody thing Mac did for her. Give the poor kid something to cheer her up. And the rest of us, come to that.' He glares at his wife.

Barbara tosses her head. 'There's no need to take that tone. I'm fed up with the way you always try to make me into the villain.'

'Give it a bloody rest —'

Julie stands up quietly and slips from the room.

*

With Allan on her side, the argument is over almost before it's begun. The following Saturday, they drive out to the airport. When Julie catches sight of Simon and Patrick Murphy in the waiting area of the HAC terminal, she has to stand behind the Crabtrees' car for a moment and hide her face in her hands. Tony must have organised it, without telling her. She'd mentioned her brilliant idea to him in passing, but she didn't know that he'd acted on it.

Simon crunches across the gravel of the car park to speak to her.

'We weren't sure if you'd still want us to come,' he says awkwardly. 'It's okay, we can always go home.

We won't be offended if you'd rather just be with the Crabtrees —'

'No, no, I'm so pleased you're here!'

Even as the words tumble from her lips, it occurs to her for the first time how weird it will be to have Simon and Ryan on the same holiday. She's not sure how Ryan will feel about it, either . . . But she's sure that she doesn't want Simon to go home.

'Dad was really touched that you'd thought of him,' Simon says.

'Is Dulcie here too?'

He shakes his head. 'No, she . . . decided not to come. But Tony did invite her. Was that because of you?'

Julie scratches at the gravel with her toe. 'Well, you know . . . of course you were all invited.'

'No *of course* about it,' says Simon. He lays his hand on her arm, and a shiver of electricity runs through her. 'I'm so sorry. About your father.'

'I feel a bit guilty,' says Julie. 'Everyone's being so kind to me, but I hardly knew him, really. He was Allan's friend for years and years . . .'

'In a way, it might make things easier for Allan, having you here,' says Simon. 'Looking after you gives him something to do. It's something he can do for your father, something useful. Does that make sense?'

'Yes.' The more Julie thinks about it, the more sense it makes. She looks at Simon with respect.

Because there are seven of them in the party, they fly in a larger plane, an Islander, with the call sign Hotel Alpha Mike. Ryan takes the seat beside Julie. 'Are you okay?'

It takes her a few seconds to work out why he's asking with such particular concern. It hasn't actually occurred to her to be frightened of flying because of what happened to Tony. Perhaps she's just stupid, or insensitive, but she honestly hasn't thought about it. 'No, I'm fine,' she says, and she lets him hold her hand, and tries to ignore the reassuring and sympathetic looks that Nadine and Barbara send in her direction.

'You sure?' says Ryan. 'You know we'll be flying right over the place where Tony went down?'

'Oh.' Julie's skin goes cold. She says, 'Yes, of course I realised that.'

Simon sits beside Patrick, who reaches across to grip Julie's hand in his strong, bony fingers.

'I was sorry to hear about Tony McGinty,' he says. 'He was a good man.'

As they fly north, Julie isn't thinking, *This is what killed my father*; she is thinking, *This is what my father loved*. The towering clouds, the roller-coaster of the air currents, the glory of the emerald-shrouded mountains and valleys laid out below, the drone of the engines speeding them through the sky, the smell of avgas and cloth seats. The view is better from the Islander than from the Baron, because the wings are attached above the windows. She stares down as the mountains rise and fall below, but she doesn't see Tony's plane.

At last the Islander begins to descend into Wewak. As Julie gazes down at the jungle, she catches sight of mysterious objects there, almost hidden by the trees. It takes her a moment to understand that she's looking at the half-rotted bodies of crashed warplanes, lying where they were shot down thirty years ago, in World War II. She covers her mouth with her hand. Beside her, Ryan picks up her other hand and squeezes it. She's aware of his eyes, liquid with anxious sympathy, too much sympathy, fixed on her face. She pulls her hand out of his grasp. For the first time, his silent concern feels oppressive rather than comforting. 'I'm okay,' she shouts, but he can't hear her. When she looks back down at the ruined planes, she can't see them any more. The Islander is sinking lower, and the trees rise up and conceal the wrecks from view.

They are staying at the Kingfisher Hotel, right on the beach. The rooms nestle in thickly thatched huts, with seagrass matting on the floors. Julie is sharing with Nadine, but as soon as she's dumped her bag on one of the beds, she is outside, two steps and onto the white sands of the beach. The sea is improbably turquoise, the sands pure and salt-white, the palm trees whispering and swaying in a benevolent line. Two seconds later, Nadine tears past her, whooping, in her bathers, and plunges into the waves. Julie sees Simon in the doorway of the next-door hut. Sudden, unreasoning happiness bubbles inside her.

'Are you coming for a swim?' she calls.

'Just getting Dad settled.' He disappears back inside, and a few minutes later he re-emerges, carrying a towel. Julie has changed into her bathers, and side by side they wade into the water; it's warm, lapping at their ankles. Julie tries not to stare at his bare chest. He is much less skinny than Ryan, filled out and muscular, probably from heaving sacks of coffee beans around all day. His skin is smooth, almost hairless, walnut brown. Once again she realises that Simon is a man, while Ryan is still a boy.

She dives into the water, pleasantly conscious that she is the most graceful swimmer among them. She grew up at the beach; for the others, it's a rare experience. They've been in the sea for about half an hour when Julie becomes aware of a figure on the sand, waving and gesticulating. She stands up, shielding her eyes from the sun. 'What's the matter? Is there a shark or something?'

Nadine lets out a melodramatic scream and falls backward into the water with a splash.

'Probably nothing.' Ryan turns away. 'Mum'll tell us if it's something important.'

Barbara is sunbathing on the sand, reading a magazine, her face hidden under a floppy hat. Simon frowns and begins to wade out, and instinctively Julie follows him. The figure on the beach reveals itself as a man, a national, wearing an official-looking cap. He speaks to Simon in Pidgin. Simon's chin thrusts up and he answers sharply.

'What is it?' says Julie. 'What's wrong?'

Simon's eyes spark with dark fire. 'He's checking that I'm a guest of the hotel. This beach is reserved for guests only.'

'But you are a guest!'

The man backs away, spreading his hands, murmuring an apology.

Julie looks at Simon. 'That's horrible. Does that — that kind of thing — does it happen a lot?'

'It won't happen after Independence,' says Simon. 'One day, all the guests in this hotel will be Papua New Guineans. No one will ever question it.' He stares along the beach.

On her towel, Barbara turns a page. She has ignored the entire scene.

'Are you coming back in?'

Simon shakes his head. 'I think I've had enough.' He splashes up onto the beach without looking back, heading for his room.

Ryan comes up behind Julie. 'Hey.' He pulls at her hand and Julie lets him drag her back a few feet into the water, until the waves are rolling past their knees. He glances around furtively. Barbara is absorbed in her magazine, Nadine busy jumping the waves. Ryan pulls Julie close and kisses her. She tastes the salt on his lips. 'Come out deeper,' he says. 'Come and swim properly. You're a great swimmer. I've been watching you.'

'No, I'm not.' But she can't help smiling. His hands are on her waist. She lets him pull her out, step by step, into deeper water, and she lets him wrap his arms around her. The warm water suspends them, embraces them. She presses her lips to his mouth. It's easier than thinking about Simon, thinking about Tony. But when Ryan slides his hands beneath the elastic of her bathers, she pulls back.

'Come on,' he says. His hands creep over her skin. 'No one can see us.'

She shakes her head; involuntarily, her eyes dart toward the beach.

Ryan gives her a little push away from him. '*He's* not looking, if that's what you're worried about.'

'I don't know what you're talking about.'

Ryan flicks his head so that his wet fringe slaps against his forehead. His eyes are narrow. Then without speaking, he turns and dives clumsily beneath the water.

Julie says, to herself, to the sky, 'I was just getting out anyway.' She begins to wade back toward the beach. Behind her, she hears Nadine shouting at Ryan, and a tremendous volley of splashing, but she knows that Ryan is still watching her.

15

Julie finds Patrick Murphy sitting on the verandah under a huge fringed umbrella. It's hotter here than in the Highlands, though a cool breeze blows off the ocean. Julie slides into a chair.

Patrick nods to the beer in front of him. 'You old enough for one of these?'

She smiles. 'Not really. I'll have a lemonade.' She leans her chin on her hand and gazes across the tranquil, sapphire-coloured sea. 'I can't believe how beautiful it is here.'

'Yes, it is beautiful. Even I can see that.' Patrick gestures to his eyes. 'They aren't what they once were. I can't see to read, these days.'

'That must be awful.'

'I won't lie to you; it's been a help having Simon home the last few weeks, doing the paperwork and what-have-you. Not looking forward to him going back to university.'

'He doesn't want to go back, you know,' says Julie. 'He wants to stay and work at Keriga.'

Patrick blinks at her and takes a long, slow sip of his beer. 'Is that right? Is that right? Well, can't blame him for that. It's God's own country up there. You coming out to visit us again?'

'I'd love to. But I think I'll be leaving soon. After — after the funeral. My mother's coming up to get me . . .' Her voice trails away. For minutes at a time, she forgets about Tony; and then, all at once, the knowledge rolls over her like a cold wave drenching her heart. After a pause, she says, 'I wish I could show my mother this place — and Keriga. She's got no idea what it's like up here.'

'Last time I was in Wewak was during the war.' Patrick closes his eyes. 'Wewak was the biggest Japanese air base in New Guinea, did you know that?'

'I saw the planes crashed in the jungle, as we flew in.'

'We lost a lot of men here,' he says.

Julie wants to ask him about the war; she wonders what he saw, what he did, if he killed anyone. She remembers what Simon told her about the violence of first contact, one side with bullets, the other side with arrows. But she doesn't know how to ask.

There is a sudden flurry as Barbara and Allan, Simon and Ryan and Nadine all arrive at once. In the bustle, Julie and Patrick become separated, and the conversation breaks off.

174

That night at dinner, Julie finds herself seated between Simon and Ryan. Ryan scowls. Julie tries not to look at Simon, but she can't help being aware of his knee, so close to hers beneath the table.

Allan taps the side of his beer glass with a fork. 'I want to propose a toast. To Mac.'

'To Mac,' everyone murmurs.

Under her breath, Julie whispers, 'To Dad.'

She'd never called him *Dad* while he was alive; they'd always preserved that slight formal distance. It's different from her mother insisting on *Caroline*, which Julie always says with an internal note of mockery, as if she were putting invisible quotes around it. She is always *Mum* really, underneath. Tony had never got to be *Dad*. And now it's too late.

Perhaps because Tony is on his mind, Allan is more short-tempered than usual. Of course, it's Allan's dinner that is delayed coming out of the kitchen, so that he's still waiting while the others sit with their meals cooling in front of them.

'Go on, start!' he barks. 'Don't let your food go stone bloody cold.'

He calls over the flustered waiter, a softly-spoken young national, and gives him a bollocking. Afterwards, Barbara says, 'It wasn't his fault.'

'It's someone's bloody fault!' roars Allan, his face

175

turning puce. Julie keeps her eyes fixed on her plate, very busy cutting up her steak.

When Allan's meal finally arrives, he pokes it with the tip of his knife. 'What the hell is this? What's this muck all over it?'

Julie keeps her head low. Beside her, Ryan is also studiously keeping his eyes turned away. At last the inevitable explosion comes. Allan pushes his plate away. 'I'm not eating this shit.' He beckons to the waiter. 'Hey, you! Take this back to the kitchen. It's bloody inedible.'

'Allan —' begins Barbara, but Allan talks over her.

'I didn't come all this way to eat crap!'

'Sir —' The waiter fumbles with a napkin. 'Let me —'

'Forget it!' Allan picks up the plate and smashes it on the floor. 'And I'm not bloody paying for it either!'

He scrapes his chair violently backward and storms from the restaurant. The young waiter, murmuring distressed apologies, nearly in tears, drops to his knees and begins trying to clear up the ruined food.

Barbara is tight-lipped. 'I'm so sorry,' she says to Patrick. 'He's been under a lot of strain.'

Patrick mutters something about no excuse for bad manners. Julie wonders why Barbara is apologising to Patrick, rather than to the waiter. She catches Simon's eye and he raises one eyebrow. Nadine is steadily eating her way through fish and chips.

'That could have been funny,' says Ryan. 'Any other time. It could have been the start of another Curry Crabtree legend . . . But not tonight.'

'It didn't seem very funny to me,' says Simon.

Barbara leans forward. 'Do you know who turned all those stories into legends? It was Tony McGinty. You know what? Without his right-hand man, Allan Crabtree is just another rude, tiresome, unfunny old bastard. Excuse my language,' she says to Patrick. 'I'm very tired. I'm going to bed.'

She pushes back her chair and stalks out.

'And then there were five,' murmurs Nadine, spearing a chip. She seems quite unperturbed by her parents' public performance.

With Allan and Barbara gone, everyone around the table seems to relax. Simon asks Nadine about boarding school; Patrick tells Julie about coffee farming. Under the table, Ryan gives Julie's knee a squeeze.

'Not sorry you came?' he whispers later, lingering outside Julie's door.

'Not sorry at all.'

The waves sigh gently up the soft sands, and the moonlight turns the sea to glowing silver. The palm trees rustle in the evening breeze. Ryan leans forward and they kiss.

He whispers in her ear, 'Want to go for a walk?'

Julie pulls away. 'I'm tired.'

'Oh. Okay.'

'See you in the morning.'

'Night.'

Ryan slouches away, shoulders slumped. Julie closes the door, and turns the lock.

*

She wakes early. There is just enough light to make out grey shapes in the room: the hump of Nadine's body in the next bed, the still shadows of the furniture. As noiselessly as she can, Julie slips out of bed and pulls on her clothes. Silently she lets herself out of the hut and walks down to the beach.

The soft, sugar-white sand is still warm from yesterday's sun. A sliver of fire shows at the horizon, bathing the pale rim of the sky with pink and gold. And then the disc of the sun slides over the edge of the sea and lights up the empty world with blue and gold and green.

Further down the beach, she can see a figure in the water, a dark head emerging above a swirl of foam. It's Simon, body-surfing. Julie hesitates, watching him as he swims. Part of her wants to walk down the beach and talk to him, but she doesn't move.

She is still standing there, watching him, when Ryan comes up behind her and grabs her hand.

'Hi. What are you doing?'

'Nothing,' she says.

'Let's get some breakfast. I'm starving.' He pulls at her hand. 'Come on.'

She's at the breakfast buffet, waiting for her toast to cook, when Simon comes up beside her. His hair is still damp from the sea, or from the shower.

'Hi.'

'Beautiful out there this morning, wasn't it?' he says.

So he did see her. 'Yes,' she says. 'It was gorgeous.'

He clears his throat. 'Julie, there's something I wanted to ask you.'

Her heart is hammering. 'Yes?'

'I don't know if your dad — if Tony was very religious? I mean, are you planning to have the funeral in a church?'

She blinks. 'I don't know. I don't think so. He and Mum got married in a registry office.'

'Because I was wondering if — the cemetery in town is a bit grim, you know? Would you like me to ask Dad, when they bring back Tony's body, if he could be buried at Keriga? Do you think he would have liked that? He'd be up in the mountains, closer to the clouds, near the sky. I mean,' he adds, 'I don't know, maybe you were planning to take his body back home with you —'

'Oh, Simon!' She is overwhelmed. She flings her arms around him, then hastily lets him go. 'Thank you! That would be — Do you think Patrick will say yes? I think Tony would have *loved* that. Could you? Could you ask him?'

'Sure, of course.' He catches her gaze and holds it. 'What's wrong?'

'Nothing.' Julie grabs a napkin and wipes her eye. 'It's just, when you said, *take him home*. Well, this is his home. This is where he'd want to stay.'

For a moment Julie wonders whether it would be such a terrible thing if they never retrieved Tony's body. Perhaps he would have preferred to be at rest inside one of the planes he loved, where he'd spent so many joyful hours, on the ground and in the air. Maybe he would have liked to be hidden in the depths of the jungle, while the wreckage slowly grew over, vines coiling through the shattered glass, tendrils knitting a canopy over the plane, and his bones sheltered inside forever ... But beautiful, peaceful Keriga would be the next best thing.

She looks at Simon. 'Thank you.'

He doesn't say a word; he just looks at her and gives a nod.

Back at the table, Ryan is twisted round in his chair, watching them. His face is like thunder.

16

When they arrive back in Mt Hagen that night, Caroline telephones for Julie. She sounds tired and harassed.

'I'm still trying to organise my visa, but I should be there some time next week, fingers crossed.'

'The funeral is supposed to be this week. A guy called Graham who lives next door is going to give the service; he's a missionary. Do you want us to wait till you get here?'

'God, no,' says Caroline. 'No, don't wait for me.'

Julie hangs up and reports the conversation to the waiting Crabtrees.

'Goodness,' says Barbara. 'It's taking a while, isn't it?'

'Give her a break, Mum,' says Ryan. 'Pretty hard to arrange anything between Christmas and New Year, everyone's on holidays.'

Barbara presses her lips together. 'Of course, Julie, you're welcome to stay with us for as long as you need to.'

'*Ryan* doesn't want you to go home,' Nadine sings out. 'Do you, Ryan?'

Ryan growls, 'Shut up, Nads.'

Abruptly Julie scrambles up and follows Allan into the kitchen, where he's dropping ice cubes into his scotch.

'Curry? I think it's time I went home. Back to the flat, I mean.'

Allan shoves the ice tray back in the freezer and slams the fridge shut. The ice cubes tinkle against his glass. 'Can't be done. You can't stay there on your own. It's not safe, you know that, look what happened last time you were there by yourself.'

'But I didn't lock up properly that time. I'd be careful —'

'No. Not going to happen.'

He gulps at his drink. Roxy begins to bark, and out in the living room Nadine calls, 'I'll get it!'

Allan cocks his head. 'Sounds like the Spargos.' He strides out to greet them. 'Heard the bottle opening, did you, Andy?'

Julie stays in the kitchen, slumped against the bench. Teddie drifts through the doorway, pulls open the fridge and peers inside. 'Beer and pickled onions . . . No, thanks . . . How are you doing, Julie? How was Wewak?'

'Lovely,' says Julie.

Teddie sticks her finger in a jar of peanut butter, and licks it thoughtfully. 'You okay?'

'I think I've outstayed my welcome here.'

'What's the problem? Barbara — no? Oh, I see. It's Ryan. Have you gone off him?'

'Ssh!' Julie casts an agonised glance at the door. 'He's . . . *nice*. But he can be a bit — you know —'

'Clingy?' Teddie screws the lid back on the jar. 'Hm. Maybe you should come and stay with me and Andy for a while.'

'Really?' Julie looks up to see if she means it. 'It wouldn't be for very long. Caroline will be here soon and then I'll be gone.' The words seem to ring through the kitchen, echoes of a beaten gong. Julie feels hollow. 'You'd better check with Andy.'

'He won't mind. He loves you. He loved Mac. He cried when Mac died. I've never seen Andy cry before. Don't tell him I told you.'

'If you're sure it's okay?' says Julie.

'Go and pack your things,' says Teddie. 'I'll tell Barbara it's our turn to have you.'

Barbara comes into Nadine's bedroom as Julie is packing. 'Of course it's up to you. If you're not comfortable here — I would have thought it would be more convenient — your mother knows you're staying here.'

'I don't want to be a nuisance,' says Julie. 'You've all been so kind.'

'It's no trouble.' Barbara, to Julie's surprise, puts her arm around her and squeezes awkwardly. 'We all have to help each other.'

Ryan carries her bag out to the car. His mouth is set in a mutinous line. 'I don't see why you have to go.'

Julie scuffs at the gravel. 'Everything just feels a bit — intense. Tony dying, and — and you and me — I think I need a bit of space, that's all.'

His face twists into a sulky frown. 'What's that supposed to mean?'

His denseness makes her want to scream. She can't explain; why can't he just understand? She knows she is being unfair. He probably thinks she's being *difficult*. But she can't help the way she feels. Guiltily she leans over and gives him a hurried kiss. 'Sorry.'

He lingers, waving, as the Spargos' car bumps down the long hibiscus-tunnel of the Crabtrees' driveway. Julie waves through the back window and turns around with a sigh. Andy is watching her through the rear-view mirror.

'He was really lovely to me, after Tony died,' falters Julie.

'Ryan's hard work, though,' says Andy. 'Even I can see that.'

*

Hunched in the armchair with the busted seat in Andy and Teddie's living room, Julie rings Caroline back to tell her that she's staying with the Spargos now. The line is muddy and there's a delay. Their voices overlap, then there's a ragged silence; they can't seem to find a rhythm. Her mother's voice is distant, muffled.

'Did you say you've moved? What for, darling?'

It's too hard to explain. Julie says helplessly, 'I just needed to, that's all.'

'But I'm coming in a few days — this wretched visa —'

Julie cuts in. 'Can you put it off, Mum? I don't want to come back yet.'

'What? I missed that —'

'I said *I don't want to come back yet*.' Julie jams her finger in her other ear. 'Can't I stay till the end of the holidays? Why can't I fly back on the ticket I've already got?'

'What was that? Where did you say you were staying?'

'With Teddie and Andy Spargo, friends of Tony's!' Julie almost shouts, conscious of Teddie and Andy sitting a few feet away in the kitchen, trying to pretend they can't hear every word she says.

'Two men? I'm not sure that's —'

'Teddie's a *girl*! They're *married*!'

'— sounds as if you don't *want* to come home —'

'No! I don't! That's what I said! You don't have to come and pick me up, like I'm a — a dog or something . . .'

'I can't hear you, sweetie —'

'That's the pips!' shouts Julie. 'I have to hang up now!' She bangs down the receiver and looks at Andy and Teddie. 'Sorry,' she says bleakly.

Teddie drapes an arm around her. 'It's all right.'

'You don't mind me being here, do you?'

'We'll tell you when we're sick of you,' says Andy with a grin, but Julie catches the quick look that flashes between him and Teddie. She stares at the rug. Of course they don't want her around for longer than a couple of days. They're practically newlyweds. They're very kind, but she can't ask them to put her up for another three or four weeks. In a small voice she says, 'I can pay rent.'

Teddie laughs and punches her shoulder. 'Don't be a dill. We don't pay anything for this place anyway, it comes with the job.'

The next day, New Year's Day, they bring Tony's body back to Hagen.

They bury him at Keriga, surrounded by mountains, high in the clouds. Early on the morning of the funeral, Teddie and Andy drive her out to the plantation. The three of them help to make sandwiches in Dulcie's kitchen. Simon introduces them, making sure they understand that this woman buttering bread at the table is not just some village meri.

'This is my mother, Dulcie.'

Teddie and Andy shake hands politely, but Julie notices that they don't seem to be able to find much to talk to her about.

Dulcie puts her arms around Julie. 'You poor little girl,' she says softly. 'It's sad to lose your *papa*. It's a sad day for you. I'm glad he's coming here to us. We look after him.'

Julie nods, and whispers, 'Thank you.'

She blinks down at the tomato she's supposed to be slicing. Despite Dulcie calling her a little girl, for the first time in her life, she feels more like an adult than a child; she is one step closer to her own death. One of her parents has died; one of the shields protecting her has fallen.

Dozens of people come out from town to attend the funeral. They stand under the sky, while Graham prays. Julie looks out over the sea of bowed heads, and she wishes fiercely that Caroline could see this. She wants to show her mother that Tony wasn't a loser or a weirdo, that he belonged here, that he was loved and honoured, that he had a place in the world. Gibbo's lank hair is scraped back in a ponytail; Allan and Ryan and Andy are wearing suits. When she sees that, she starts to cry.

Robyn hugs her. 'We're so, so sorry, honey,' she murmurs. 'He was just an adorable man.'

So many people hug Julie that day, her ribs feel bruised.

After the service, Julie finds herself alone in a corner of the wide verandah. She isn't exactly trying to hide from Ryan, but she doesn't think she can face his smothering sympathy. And she definitely doesn't want anyone to try to kiss her, not today. The mountains seem much nearer here, a blue haze rising over them like smoke. Simon comes up, carrying a cup of tea. 'I thought you might need this.'

'Thanks.' Julie takes a grateful sip, and almost chokes.

'I should have warned you, there's a slug of brandy in it. Dad's idea.'

'I think I just need to get used to it . . .' Julie sips again, and the brandy travels like a trail of fire down her throat, and curls in a warm pool in her stomach.

Out on the lawn below the verandah, guests mill about, dispersing, waving solemn goodbyes. They are going back to their cars, back to town, back to their lives. Julie swallows. She is the only one with nothing to go back to.

Simon leans his arms on the railing and stares down at them. 'So, I guess you'll be leaving soon.'

'My mother will be here in a couple of days.' Julie sets down her cup. 'I wish I didn't have to go. I wish I could stay until the end of the holidays, like we planned.'

'Why don't you?'

'I can't keep staying with the Spargos. I mean, they've been great, but they don't want me hanging around forever. And I don't want to stay with the Crabtrees. But Curry won't let me go back to Tony's flat on my own . . .'

There is a silence. Julie thinks, *Ask me to stay with you; ask me to stay here.* It seems so much the obvious thing for Simon to say that she is almost embarrassed for him.

But instead he says slowly, 'You know, you probably can't stay on now. You don't have a valid visa any more, now that Tony's gone.'

This news startles her. It hasn't occurred to her that her continued presence here might actually be illegal. 'But — they wouldn't kick me out, would they?'

Simon shrugs. 'They're pretty strict on visas.' He says it apologetically, as if he's a member of the government himself.

'But no one's going to *know*, are they? Are they?'

'I don't know. I don't know how they police it.'

'Why would they care?'

'I don't know.' Simon gives her an apologetic smile. He says abruptly, 'Come and see my pigeons.'

Julie sets down her cup and saucer on the railing and follows him. Her feet are like lead. Why hasn't he invited her to stay, even knowing that she might be — what was the word? — *deported* at any moment? His silence bruises her. She trails after him through the shabby, rambling house, out through the kitchen. They pass a lovingly tended vegetable garden and some sheds. Julie stumbles on, hardly noticing where she's walking. Above her head, the clouds roll over themselves, folding like egg whites into the blue batter of the sky. Pigeons. Who keeps pigeons? Old men on rooftops. Lonely old men . . .

'Here they are.' Simon halts beside an aviary of tin and chicken wire.

Julie peers inside. Several goose-sized birds the blue-grey-purple colour of the hazy mountains are strutting about. Each one carries a crest on top of its head, a fan of lacy feathers, each feather tipped with a blue-and-white eye, like a peacock's tail.

She forgets that she's upset with Simon. 'They're beautiful . . . But they're not *pigeons*!'

'Yes, they are. Big ones. They're Victoria Crowned Pigeons.' Simon coos softly to the birds and they turn toward him. Carefully he eases open the aviary door and tosses in a handful of seeds. 'They're kind of rare. I've been breeding them.' He closes the door. 'It's not easy. They're very faithful; they mate for life. And they're very intelligent.'

'Because they mate for life?'

'I'd say that was an intelligent thing to do. Make a good choice and stick to it.'

Julie sneaks a look at him, but he's not looking at her; his eyes are fixed steadily on the birds.

'They're lovely,' she says. 'I can see why you like them. But they're so *big*.'

'Related to the dodo, actually. The dodo was a kind of pigeon. The dodo was much bigger than these, though. More meat on the bones.'

'I think I've seen those feathers.'

Simon nods. 'They look good in headdresses. That's one reason why they're getting rarer.' He falls silent; Julie has never heard him talk so much, except when he was explaining the coffee business. Even on the night when they'd had that long phone call, she'd ended up doing most of the talking.

She tangles her fingers in the wire and stares at the birds. 'Can they fly?'

'Oh, yeah, they can fly.'

'They can't fly inside there.'

'No.' He gives her a sad smile. 'That's the price for keeping them safe.'

'But they don't understand that.'

'I said they were intelligent. But maybe not that intelligent.'

Julie watches as the birds peck and murmur. She still doesn't understand why Simon won't invite her to stay at Keriga. She is intelligent, but not that intelligent.

She stands beside Simon, so close that their fingers, interlaced in the wire, are almost touching; so close that she can feel the heat coming off his body, and smell his aftershave. And even though she's decided that she doesn't want to be kissed on this day, she thinks, if Simon turns his head — if he moves his mouth toward her — she just might be able to make an exception.

Simon steps back. The wire of the cage shakes as he removes his hands.

'We'd better get back. They'll be looking for you.'

Julie hears herself say, 'When you say *they*, do you mean Ryan?'

He has a guarded expression on his face. 'I didn't say anything about Ryan.'

'Oh. Okay. Never mind.'

'I was thinking of Andy Spargo. They're driving you back, aren't they?'

'Yes. Yes, of course.'

She follows him back to the house, careful to stay behind him, so that he can't see the furious red that flushes in her cheeks.

17

It's time to clear out the unit. Everyone has an opinion.

'Think you're up to it?' Allan says heavily.

'I can take care of it,' says Barbara. 'Leave it to me.'

'Do you want me to come and help?' offers Teddie. 'Or just keep you company?'

'Graham and I can help you out, honey,' says Robyn. 'We're praying for you.'

'I could have a crack at it,' says Gibbo. 'Get you started. Better to be a diamond with a flaw, than a pebble without.'

But Julie tells them all, 'I'd rather do it alone.'

'If that's the way you want it,' says Allan. 'It's up to you. It's all yours, you know. You're his next of kin, his only child. There's life insurance, too. That'll come to you.'

Julie nods, silenced by the lump in her throat. Money, life insurance, inheritance. It all seems meaningless and unreal. But Tony's possessions, in his home, the bits and pieces of his everyday life, his clothes and plates and records — they are real. She owes it to him to take care of his things. In a strange way, this will be the last time she gets to spend with the man who was her father. She doesn't want anyone else there, getting in the way, filling up the space with chat. She wants to finish the job before Caroline arrives. She is relieved when Ryan doesn't even offer to help.

'Well, if you're absolutely sure,' says Barbara over the phone. 'Don't bother about cleaning the place. When you're finished, I'll send Koki around to take care of all that.'

'There's no need —'

But Barbara has already hung up.

*

When Julie lets herself inside the unit, it's exactly as she left it, almost two weeks ago. The dishes from her last meal are unwashed and crusty in the sink; a coffee cup with a deep brown ring still sits on the bench. Fruit has rotted in the bowl. The musty smell and the rich, sour odour of decay wash over her. For a second, she is tempted to ring Barbara and hand over the responsibility to her, but then she straightens herself up. Everything in this flat belongs to her, Allan said. It's up to her to decide what to do with it; it's her job, her last duty to her father.

She flings all the doors wide and yanks open the window louvres in every room, pulls back the curtains and lets the sun flood in. Clouds of dust motes dance in the disturbed air. Then she gathers up all the food that's gone off, from the fruit bowl and the fridge, and dumps it all on the compost heap at the bottom of the garden.

The next job, because it's the easiest, is to go to her room and pack her own suitcase. There isn't much there, because she'd taken most of her things to Teddie and Andy's in her overnight bag that first night when Tony went missing. There are a couple of books, some clothes she wasn't wearing anyway — a spare pair of jeans, the thick jumper Caroline had insisted on — and a few stray toiletries in the bathroom, her shampoo and conditioner. It doesn't take long to shove everything into her suitcase.

Julie stands in the centre of her room. She gazes at the Holly Hobbie poster, the girl in the bonnet, her face turned away: the picture that Tony had so carefully fastened to the wall to make the room pretty and cosy for her, when he was expecting, somehow, a younger daughter. A sob closes around Julie's throat like a tightening hand. She peels the poster down and carefully creases it and lays it in the bottom of her suitcase, buried beneath everything else, flat and safe.

Sorting out Tony's clothes isn't too painful. Because she's known Tony for such a short time, there are few memories attached to the things he's worn. He has

195

hardly any casual clothes — a couple of loud shirts, a pair of slacks, baggy shorts. Barbara had suggested putting those aside, along with the sheets and towels and kitchen equipment, for Robyn and Graham to distribute through the mission. The underwear drawer she sweeps into a garbage bag, for the incinerator. No one wants to wear a dead man's Y-fronts. A picture flashes unbidden into her mind, of Tony's red jocks beneath a *laplap* and *arse-gras*, and a snort of laughter bursts out of her.

And then all that's left is his pilot's uniform — the crisp white shirts that he ironed himself every Sunday night, the dark shorts, the cap with the HAC badge that she's never seen one of Allan's pilots actually wear. All this goes in a box, for Gibbo and Andy, if they'll fit. Tony's epaulettes and his wings, retrieved by Allan from the body, Julie has already set aside to keep.

He has hardly any books. Julie finds *Jonathan Livingston Seagull* — flying, of course — and a copy of *Chariots of the Gods*. There are spy stories and books about aeroplanes and war, and a collection of Pidgin phrasebooks. Well hidden in a box under the bed are some copies of *Playboy*, which Julie leafs through curiously at first, then drops, feeling slightly sick. Quite likely Ryan might appreciate those, but they go into the incinerator bag. The spy novels she puts aside for Simon.

She tucks the Pidgin phrasebooks and dictionaries into her suitcase, as well as one of the flying instruction manuals.

On top of the wardrobe, thickly coated with dust, she finds a model battleship. She lifts it gently down with both hands. It must have taken months to build. Every gun turret, every miniature railing, every lifeboat has been meticulously constructed, carved from balsa and glued painstakingly into position. He must have laboured over it night after night, in a pool of light at the kitchen table, while the flying ants bumbled into the globe. The ship is carefully painted, with only the slightest wobble of a stripe or a stray brush-hair to show that he did the job by hand. It's light in her hands, floating in the air as it would on water, perfectly balanced, sweet and true. It's magnificent, labour and craftsmanship to be proud of. But when it was finished, he shoved it on top of the wardrobe, as if he was ashamed, ashamed, perhaps, of the lonely nights that produced it.

Julie doesn't know what to do with the battleship. She can't bear to think of destroying it. She lays it on the table, where it must have sat during all the hours and months when Tony was working on it, and leaves it there.

She lifts down the giant carved shield from the wall. It's hung there so long, the paint is a different colour behind it. She wishes she could take it home with her, but it's far too big to smuggle into her hand luggage. Then there's the fistful of spears, fanned out on another wall, and a penis gourd. Tony had put that in a cupboard before she arrived. She's definitely not taking *that* back to Australia.

She picks up a wooden lamp base, carved into two faces, with shells set into it to make blind eyes. The two faces look rather like forbidding Easter Island heads, frowning grimly. On one side of the base, a flaw in the wood makes it look as if a dribble of snot is escaping from his nose. It's as ugly as hell, but somehow Julie feels perversely affectionate toward it. Surely this guy will fit in her suitcase.

As she weighs it in her hands, something wobbles on its underside. She turns it over and works with her fingertips, and a section of the base comes loose, revealing a hollow space inside. Julie reaches in, her heart thumping, and draws out a tightly wadded roll of banknotes, secured with a rubber band. The bundle of colourful Australian notes falls apart in her hands, orange for twenties, the new yellow fifties, like autumn leaves. She is holding about five hundred dollars in her lap; it's more cash than she's ever seen in her entire life. And it's hers.

She doesn't know what to do; she stares at the money, mesmerised. At last she rolls it up again, stuffs the bundle inside a pair of socks, and thrusts it deep in her shoulder bag. Some instinct warns her to keep this secret.

In the bottom drawer in Tony's bedroom, she finds a single photo album. If only she'd known about this before he died! If only they could have spent an evening together, sitting on the couch, while he told her the stories behind the photographs — the friends he'd made, the places he'd seen, some of those funny stories like the ones he'd wheeled out at the Crabtrees' dinner table. She could have taken notes, made labels . . .

She flip opens the album. Then she sinks onto the bed. This isn't the book of Tony's life. It's her own.

Inside this volume, neatly arranged, is a copy of every school photo: Julie with a gap-toothed smile, Julie with a freckled nose, Julie with pigtails, with a fringe, with a single ponytail, smiling, frowning, eyes sliding away from the camera, growing older with every photo, her cheeks thinning out, her eyes more serious. And there are other photos of her, too, dutifully slipped inside Christmas cards by Caroline: on the swing in their backyard, sitting on Nana's steps, under the Christmas tree unwrapping a box of Lego. And in the back of the album, arranged chronologically, is wedged every carelessly scrawled Christmas card and note that Caroline had made her write, each year, to the distant stranger who was her father.

Reading them now, they seem so perfunctory, so thoughtless, each word is like a blow. *Dear Tony, Happy Christmas. We went to Luna Park. It was fun. From Julie. Dear Tony, I hope you are well. We are well. School is okay. Next door have a new baby, he cries a lot! Well, that's all. Have a merry Christmas! From Julie.* Each one filed, dated and tucked away.

Why hadn't she ever bothered to write him a proper letter? And why hadn't he ever written one to her? Or sent her a present? Never anything for Christmas, nothing for her birthday. She's always assumed, and Caroline has encouraged her to assume, that he just wasn't interested, that he didn't care. But now she realises the truth: he was too shy. Too afraid of sending her the wrong thing, of saying the wrong words, and so he'd stayed silent. Also, there aren't many shops up here. Maybe he was afraid that whatever he could buy at the market, or one of the Chinese trade stores, or at Carpenters or Beeps, wouldn't be good enough. Safer to send nothing at all.

At least she knows that now; at least they had these few short weeks. What if she hadn't come? What if she'd never met him at all? How would she have felt when Caroline got the letter, or the phone call from Allan? Would she have cared? She would have felt important, swollen with drama, for a month or so. *My father's died. My father's plane crashed. My father was killed in New Guinea.* But it wouldn't have seemed real; it wouldn't have been real. This — this twisting of her heart, this ache in her throat — it's horrible, but she's glad, glad to feel it.

Beneath the photo album is a large envelope with a manila folder inside. Perhaps this will be her school reports, or copies of her best projects; who knows what Caroline sent to him.

But what falls out onto the mattress is a jumble of papers — letters, receipts, carbon copies of official-looking forms. Julie shuffles through them, bewildered. There is a report card — and another — but not from her school. This doesn't make sense. The reports are from a school in Goroka. The name on the top of the card reads *Helen McGinty*.

Julie stares at the words until they begin to dance before her eyes. Then, feverishly, she grabs at the letters, the bills, the receipts, scanning them for clues. The bills are from the same school. Tony has been paying the fees. The latest receipt is from only a couple of months ago. Julie shakes the envelope and a small black-and-white snapshot falls out. It's a girl, about ten or eleven, staring into the camera. Her hair is thick and curling, tied with a ribbon; her skin is dark. Julie turns the photo over. The back is blank. But she doesn't need a label to tell her that this girl is Helen. Helen McGinty.

She must be Tony's daughter. Tony's other daughter. Julie's half-sister.

18

For a moment she sits motionless. Her head is swimming; she thinks she might pass out.

Then, with a single clumsy gesture, she sweeps all the papers, the photo, the letters, back into the big yellow envelope. She flies from window to door, locking up. She slings her bag over her shoulder and picks up her suitcase. She finds herself on the front steps, gazing at Tony's keys in her hand, as if she's never seen a bunch of keys before. Tony's little white car sits in the driveway, waiting.

Her hands shake as she inserts the key in the car door. For a second she thinks the engine won't start, but it coughs and turns over, and the car jumps as she sorts out clutch and gears and accelerator and brake, Caroline's lessons flooding back into her mind. She backs out of the driveway and swerves onto the road. Head check, head check. And she's forgotten her seatbelt ... but the cars up here don't have seatbelts. She can't find the indicator. The windscreen wipers slash madly across the glass, and the gears grind as she wrestles with the stick.

It's been a while since her last lesson, and the bumpy Mt Hagen roads are a long way from the quiet suburban crescents of bayside Melbourne.

But soon she's out on the highway, on the way to Keriga. She has to concentrate so hard on driving that there's no room in her mind for her discovery: that girl, the secret envelope. She has to get to Simon; she has to tell him. He'll know what to do. A car comes speeding toward her and instinctively she swerves out of the way — too far — as it shoots past, then swings violently back into the middle of the road. *Calm down, Julie.* Now the image of the girl comes bubbling back up. She can't breathe. She gropes for the handle to crank down the window and gulps in mouthfuls of cool air. A sister, a New Guinean sister. Who is her mother? Why didn't Tony ever mention her? Does Allan Crabtree know about her? No, he can't — he said, *you're Tony's only child, his next of kin . . .*

With a start, she realises she's about to drive past the Keriga turnoff. Just in time she yanks at the steering wheel and gravel sprays beneath the tyres. Too fast, too fast — desperately she hauls at the wheel with one hand and shoves at the gearstick with the other. She's spinning, the car is spinning, someone is shouting, swearing, and a tree rears up before her. With one final frantic effort she slams at the brake and drags at the wheel, and the car swings about, bumps once, twice, with a jolt that flings her sideways, and stops. Julie's forehead is squashed against the steering wheel. There is a terrible blaring noise. She fumbles with the key and manages to switch off the ignition. She realises she's leaning against the horn, and hastily rears back. The blaring stops abruptly; the silence that follows seems almost as deafening. The car is in the ditch, its front corner crumpled. That was her own voice, shouting obscenities . . . She giggles weakly, and the giggle becomes a sob. She can't move, can't think. Her cheeks are wet, her eyes leaking tears. She leans her arms on the wheel, leans her head on her arms, and closes her eyes.

Perhaps she even falls asleep for a minute.

A sudden sharp tapping near her ear makes her jump out of her skin.

A dark face is peering in the window. She bites back the urge to scream. Then she sees that it's Moses, the Keriga foreman. She winds down the window. 'Hello.'

He looks worried. 'You all right, misis?'

'Not really.' She gives him a wobbly smile. 'I seem to have crashed my car.'

He wrenches at the car door and forces it open, then holds out his large, comforting hand. 'You come.'

Moses carries her suitcase, but Julie clutches the yellow envelope and her shoulder bag tightly to her body. Her knees won't stop shaking, so she also has to cling to Moses's arm. It feels like a rod of steel. All the way to the house, he talks to her, a stream of murmurous reassurance that she hears but barely understands, a mixture of English and Pidgin and maybe something else. Simon has told her that most nationals speak two or three languages before they learn Pidgin. What language does her sister speak? She has lost a father and found a sister. She feels delirious.

Moses helps her up the steps, calling for Dulcie. Dulcie comes hurrying out, takes one look at Julie and gently pushes her into a chair, exclaiming in concern. Dulcie and Moses have an agitated conversation, with much shrugging from Moses, and at last he jogs down the steps and away across the grass.

It's not until Dulcie fetches a bowl of water and a cloth that Julie realises she's cut her head; blood is sticky behind her ear, oozing through her hair. She winces as Dulcie gently sponges at the cut. 'I crashed the car,' she tells Dulcie.

Dulcie clucks absently. 'You sit there. I make you a cup of tea.'

Julie sits, gingerly touching her scalp. Inside the house, she can hear Patrick's querulous voice, and Dulcie soothing him.

Simon comes bounding up the steps. 'Julie? Moses

told me you crashed a car! What the hell were you doing driving out here?'

'I've got my learners,' says Julie. 'I can drive.'

Simon raises his eyebrows. 'Apparently. But if you wanted to come for a visit, I could have picked you up.'

Julie says, 'I found something.'

She finds she can't look at him; she's staring at the floor. Her throat is tight.

Simon draws up a chair beside her. 'Tell me.'

Wordless, she hands him the envelope. Frowning, he sorts through the contents, and she sees comprehension dawn on his face. He looks up.

'I think I know who her mother was,' she says. 'Tony used to have a meri when he first came up here. He said it didn't work out.'

'Hm,' says Simon. 'There are quite a few meri and employer situations that *don't work out* like that. At least he seems to have taken responsibility for the baby, even given her his name. There aren't many expats who'd do that.'

Your father did. But she doesn't say it. 'We would never have known about Tony and this girl if he hadn't died. It was all a big secret.' Julie looks at him in anguish. 'She doesn't know he's died. We have to tell her. And who's going to pay her school fees now?' She jumps up. 'I need to find her. I need to get to Goroka.

Can you help me get the car out of the ditch? It's not far to Goroka, is it? Could I drive there?'

'It's possible to drive there,' says Simon. 'But you're not doing it. Sit down. You're in shock.'

Dulcie brings out a mug of tea. It's hot and sweet. As Julie sips at it, she can hear Simon and his mother having a murmured conference in the doorway behind her.

Simon sits down again. 'Listen, Julie. We have to ring the Crabtrees, tell them where you are.'

'I'm not staying with them any more. I'm at Andy and Teddie Spargo's house.'

'Okay, then we'll call them. They can come and pick you up.'

'No — no, no, I have to go to Goroka. I have to find Helen.'

Saying her name makes it seem more real. She can almost see the anxious little girl, sitting on the end of a boarding school bed, her hands folded, waiting to hear her fate. Waiting for Julie . . . Does Helen know that she has a sister? 'I can't just leave her there. Please, Simon.'

He runs his hand over his head. 'You've only got the address of this school, right? She won't even be there, Julie. It's the holidays.'

'She might be there. Some kids stay at boarding school for the holidays, don't they?'

'Yes,' he has to admit. 'Sometimes.'

'The school is the only clue we have. There's nothing else, no phone number, no home address ... Please, Simon! I can drive there. I've calmed down now. Look.' She holds out her hand, flat, to show him how steady it is. Unfortunately it's trembling like a *guria* shaking a house.

Simon grabs her hand and presses it between his own. Her heart flips over. 'You can't drive anywhere,' he says firmly.

Julie says faintly, 'If you don't let me, I'll sneak out in the middle of the night.'

'Moses says your car is too wrecked to drive.'

'Then I'll take Andy's car. All I have to do is drive along the Highlands Highway, don't I? Goroka's the next town.'

'It's a four-hour drive!'

'I don't care. My mother will be here soon; I'll have to go home. This is my last chance. *Please*, Simon! If I don't look after her, nobody will. She's my family ... She's my wontok.'

'Julie —' He shakes his head, smiling. He's still holding onto her hand. 'All right,' he says, and sighs. 'You win.'

'You mean I can take the car?'

'No! You can't drive to Goroka.' He lets go of her hand, abruptly, as if he's just realised that he's holding it. 'I'll take you.'

209

19

Patrick won't let them leave until Julie has rung Teddie at HAC and told her that she's safe, and not to worry.

'I'm staying with the Murphys tonight,' says Julie, winding the phone cord around her finger. 'Maybe two nights.'

She tells herself it's not really a lie — after all, she will be with Simon.

'Okay,' says Teddie distractedly. The other phone line is ringing. 'Have fun . . .'

As Julie hangs up, she feels slightly indignant that Teddie hasn't questioned her more closely. But then a liberating lightness washes through her; she is free. She can go wherever she likes. She is going to find her sister, and no one can stop her.

She says to Simon, 'Let's go.'

They take the Jeep. 'It would be much quicker to fly, you know,' says Simon.

'No,' says Julie. 'I don't want to do that.'

'More expensive,' agrees Simon.

But it's not the expense; Julie knows that she couldn't fly anywhere in New Guinea without Allan Crabtree finding out about it. She doesn't know if the Crabtrees would try to stop her on this quest, but she doesn't want to take any chances. Tony had kept Helen secret; for now, Julie figures she should do the same.

'What are you going to do, if you find her?'

'We *will* find her,' says Julie. 'I know we will.'

'And?'

Julie is silent for a moment. 'Tell her about Tony. Tell her I'm her sister. She needs to know that I'll look after her, that I'm her family now.'

A burst of rain sweeps over them. Simon turns on the windscreen wipers, and as Julie watches their hypnotic arc, she finds her eyelids growing heavy.

When she snaps awake again, the road looks different. The trees have thinned out, the slope of the mountain dropping away to one side. The rain has stopped, and the valley floor spreads out in a sunlit vista, as brightly and improbably green as a lime spider.

'Sorry.'

'That's okay. You looked like you needed it.'

'I wasn't snoring, was I?'

'Oh, no. Not at all.'

'Good.'

There is a pause. Simon says, 'You were drooling, though.'

'I wasn't!' She stares at him in horror.

'Just a little bit.'

He grins, and she realises how rare it is to see him smile. Suddenly self-conscious, she shifts in her seat. One of her feet has gone to sleep, and she rubs it, grimacing, as pins and needles take hold.

'How far have we got to go?'

'Hours yet. I hope we get there before dark. Not much fun driving this road at night.'

'Sorry,' says Julie.

'That's okay. I volunteered, remember?'

A truck, laden with passengers, rattles past them, and Simon veers aside to let them pass. A fleck of gravel flies up and strikes the windscreen, and Julie can't help flinching. She hopes Simon hasn't noticed. Dulcie has packed them a basket of food, but she is too nervous to eat. She keeps trying to picture her first meeting with Helen, but her imagination seems to shut down; she can't push the scene beyond *Hello, I'm Julie* . . .

The road twists and turns through the mountains. Julie glances out at dizzying drops and hastily looks away, wondering why crawling along the ground is more frightening than flying miles above it.

'Shit,' says Simon softly.

'What? What's the matter?'

Julie sits up in alarm, peering ahead. She sees an old, battered car slewed across the narrow road, blocking the way ahead, and a couple of men lounging against it. 'Have they broken down?'

'I doubt it,' says Simon grimly. 'Lock your door, Julie.'

Her heart begins to hammer. She snaps down the lock and pushes her shoulder bag out of sight beneath the seat, as Simon slows the Jeep and pulls up near the parked vehicle. He keeps the engine idling as he winds down the window and leans casually out. '*Wanem, yupela?*'

The two men push themselves off from the car and saunter across. One of them rests his bum on the bonnet; his weight makes the Jeep sag. The other one jumps up onto the running board, so his face is level with Simon's. He grins, showing betel-stained teeth. He has a machete thrust through his belt.

Julie tries to keep her face neutral. But her heart is pounding as she sees one, two, three more men emerge from the trees, detaching themselves from the dappled shadows. They stand motionless in the road, watching. The jungle folds around them all like a smothering cloak, dark, damp, and choking.

These are the raskols she's heard so much about. For a fleeting moment, she wonders what might have happened if she'd driven this road by herself, as she'd wanted to. Thank God she is with Simon.

But then she realises that this isn't over. It hasn't even begun. There are five of them, standing around the car, relaxed, loose-limbed, confident. One of them picks his teeth with the tip of a knife. Simon leans out through the window, apparently just as relaxed as they are. But he keeps the engine running. Menace hangs in the air like the thrumming echo of a war cry.

She wants to whisper to Simon that she has some money. Could she extract a couple of notes without letting them see the whole roll of cash? She is so conscious of the bundle in the bag under her seat, she can't believe the raskols don't sense it too. The man's powerful smell fills the car: tobacco and musk and grease and sweat.

Simon and the chief raskol are speaking. Julie can't follow their rapid patter of Pidgin, back and forth — is it even Pidgin? It's too fast to tell. She sits upright, on the edge of her seat, taut as a guitar string. Could she make a run for it? Crash off into the bush and hide? She dismisses the idea instantly; they would catch her at once. Does Simon have a weapon — a gun?

For the first time in New Guinea, she is truly frightened. Her palms are slippery with sweat, and cold as ice.

The chief raskol's right hand rests lightly on the machete in his belt. He is frowning. Now Simon is reaching into his back pocket.

'Simon?' Her voice is a squeak.

'It's okay.' He doesn't look at her; his gaze is fixed steadily on the face of the man leering through the open window. As Julie watches, he pulls out his wallet and plucks out a ten-dollar note. It vanishes into the raskol's fist as if sucked up a vacuum tube. The man is still frowning. He says something: demanding more. Simon shakes his head. The raskol's fist thuds into the side of the Jeep, and Julie jumps. Slowly, reluctantly, Simon pulls out another note — a five this time. He shows the raskol his empty wallet, shrugs and grimaces. Frowning, the raskol accepts the five-dollar note. It's as if he's turning over possibilities in his mind.

Julie holds her breath. Rapidly she runs over Caroline's self-defence lessons in her mind, the list of vulnerable places to target if she's attacked — the throat, the crotch, the top of the foot. Could she grab the machete? She remembers the axe-blade scar on Tony's head. She remembers the promise she made to him: *Don't do anything silly* . . . It was almost the last conversation they ever had. Her eyes blur with sudden tears.

And then, at last, the raskol smacks his palm on the Jeep's bonnet. He yells something over his shoulder, and the car blocking their way begins to inch aside. Julie hadn't even noticed the driver at the wheel, waiting for his orders. Simon quickly winds up the window and shoves at the gear stick. The Jeep rolls forward; the chief raskol jumps out of the way. The car in front jerks back and forth. 'Come on, come on,' mutters Simon. His hands grip the wheel. The raskols yell at each other, flinging their hands in the air.

As soon as there is room to pass, Simon throws the Jeep into gear and the vehicle shoots forward through the gap. Then they are roaring away, bumping from side to side as the Jeep hurtles down the road.

Julie lets out the breath she's been holding. 'What did you say to them?'

'Not much. Asked them where they were from. Figured out he was one of my wontoks, luckily, that's why they let us go.'

'Did you have to give them all your money?'

Simon laughs. 'Most of my cash is in my pocket. The wallet was just for show, in case something like this happened.'

'I'll pay you back,' says Julie.

'Don't worry about it.'

She sneaks a sideways look at him. He is frowning ahead, his profile set and stern. Suddenly he looks completely New Guinean; she can't find a trace of

Patrick, or any European, in his face. He is one of them, a wontok; this is his world, the world of haggling and payback, village obligations and village justice. These negotiations are as much a part of him as the world of the boarding school cricket team and model aeroplanes and reading Graham Greene.

Julie looks away, at the blurred reel of bush unscrolling past the window. It's beginning to rain again, the heavy drops pelting against the glass. She feels safe, closed inside the Jeep, with Simon beside her. She wriggles down in her seat and closes her eyes.

20

Without consciously thinking about it, Julie is half-expecting Simon to take the lead when they find the school at last. He is the man; he's older than she is; he's taller; he's the driver. But as they walk up to the door of the low fibro building, Simon drops back to let Julie go ahead of him, and it's Julie who raps on the door.

They wait.

'Maybe there's no one here,' says Julie. 'It is the holidays.'

Part of her wants to seize any excuse to turn and run; her stomach is churning.

'Someone's coming,' says Simon.

The door creaks open. A slightly built white woman peers out at them through round, wire-rimmed spectacles. 'Yes? Can I help you?'

Julie's mouth is dry. 'We're trying to find Helen McGinty. I think she's a student here?'

'Oh, yes.' The woman opens the door a little wider and her face relaxes into a smile. She looks over Julie's shoulder at Simon. 'You're family, I take it?'

'Yes,' says Julie.

'She's not here at the moment, the boarding school's closed over Christmas. Helen spends the holidays with one of the teachers, Miss Elliot. Wait there a moment, I can give you the address.'

The woman retreats swiftly away down the corridor, and returns with an address scribbled on a scrap of paper. 'Down past the airport, turn right at Griffiths Street.'

'Wow,' says Julie, slightly dazed, as she and Simon climb back into the Jeep. 'That was easy.'

'So far,' says Simon. He reverses the Jeep out of the car park. 'Now comes the hard part.'

Goroka is a larger town than Mt Hagen, better laid out and more attractive, with well-tended gardens and more established houses. 'People stay here longer than they do in Hagen,' says Simon. 'Hagen's still a frontier town. There are a lot more expats in Goroka.'

He pulls up the Jeep in front of a house on stilts, surrounded by poinsettia bushes. A small green car is parked underneath the house; a washing line, hung with tea towels, is strung between the supporting struts. Julie opens her door, then looks back at Simon, who hasn't moved. 'You're coming with me, aren't you?'

'Maybe I should stay here.'

'Why?'

Simon sighs and opens his door. 'Okay, I'll come.'

Again he lets Julie go first as they stump up the stairs to the front door. Julie clutches her shoulder bag with the yellow envelope inside. Can it really be only this morning that she found it? Now the day is almost over; the sky is beginning to grow dark. Julie pulls open the fly screen and knocks at the door. She can hear music playing inside — a pop song. It might be 'You're So Vain'.

The music stops abruptly, and Julie hears footsteps crossing the floor. She tries to swallow, but her throat is dry. Nervously she tucks her hair behind her ears.

The door cracks open, and a brown eye peers out at them.

'Hello,' says Julie. 'Are you Helen?'

The door opens wider. A girl, about the same age as Nadine, perhaps a little younger, twelve or thirteen, wearing a neat blue-and-white cotton dress, stands with her hands barring the doorway. Her hair is thick and dark and straight, smoothed back from her forehead. A tiny apple hairclip gleams behind each ear. She stares mistrustfully out at Simon and Julie. Her skin is a shade darker than Simon's.

'Yes, I'm Helen,' she says in a low voice.

'Helen McGinty?' Julie's voice trembles.

'Yes.'

Julie holds out her hand. 'My name is Julie McGinty. I think I'm your sister.'

The girl's face goes blank, a curtain drawn across. She does not move.

Simon says, 'Is your teacher here? Miss Elliot?'

The girl's head turns, and she calls to someone in the house behind her. She is still holding onto the doorjamb, blocking the entrance, as if she thinks they will storm in and trample her.

Miss Elliot appears behind Helen's shoulder. Julie feels a slight shock as she sees that the teacher is a national, or more likely mixed-race, her skin golden-brown, sprinkled with a smattering of darker freckles, her fuzzy hair springing out in an afro around her head. She's young, only a little older than Simon. She wears jeans and a meri blouse. She stares out at Julie and Simon with a puzzled frown.

'I think perhaps we'd better come inside,' says Simon.

Miss Elliot moves in front of Helen with a protective motion. She says, 'I'm sorry, who are you?'

'She says she's my sister.' Helen flickers her dark eyes at Julie. 'I'm sorry, I've forgotten your name.'

'This is Julie McGinty,' says Simon. 'And my name is Simon Murphy, I'm a friend.'

Slowly Miss Elliot stands aside. 'Okay. Maybe you should come in.'

The house is comfortably messy; books are scattered about, a cardigan dropped on the back of a chair, a pair of clogs kicked off beside the door. There's a Van Gogh poster on one wall. With a pang, Julie thinks of her own untidy home, with Caroline, back in Melbourne.

'Now,' says Miss Elliot severely, in a teacher's voice. 'What is all this about, please?'

But Julie is already shaking out the contents of the yellow envelope onto the dining table. Report cards skid onto the floor and Julie clumsily snatches them up. Helen moves a wooden fruit bowl aside to make more room; her face is expressionless.

'This is you, isn't it? Your school bills — your reports — and this photo? I mean, you're older, obviously — in real life, I mean, not in the photo —' Julie hears herself gabbling, breathless. Of course it's Helen. She's started in the wrong place. She takes a deep breath and tries to catch Helen's eye, to look at her directly. But Helen is staring down at the table; she won't look at her.

'Listen,' says Julie. 'Your father's Tony McGinty, right? Well, he was my father, too.'

At that Helen does look up. 'Was?'

There is a silence.

Simon says gently, 'I'm sorry, Helen. We have some bad news for you.'

'He's dead,' blurts Julie, before she can stop herself. Without warning, tears sting her eyes and she has to turn away. In a muffled voice she goes on, 'It was just before Christmas . . . He was flying from Koinambe to Mt Hagen . . . His plane crashed. The weather was really bad — he shouldn't have taken off, probably — he was usually very careful — he crashed in the Jimi Valley. You know he was a pilot? Yes, of course you do . . .'

She is rambling again.

There is another silence. Miss Elliot crosses the room to put her arm around Helen's shoulders.

Helen says, 'I didn't know him.' Her voice is flat and small. She picks up the tiny photo of herself from the table and stares at it as if it were the face of a stranger. Then a flash of fear crosses her face, and she turns to Simon. She says, 'He paid for my school. Who will pay my school fees now?'

Simon clears his throat. 'Well . . .'

'I will!' Julie says. 'I'm your big sister. Tony was my father, too. We're sisters; I'll look after you. You can come back to live in Australia with me, you can go to my school. It's perfect, we have a spare room in our house — We could *adopt* you!'

'Hold on a second,' says Simon.

'My mum will say yes, I know she will! She always wants to help people.' But Julie's voice wavers.

'I don't want to go to Australia.' Helen's voice rises, her dark eyes widen in panic.

'No one's going to make you do anything you don't want to do,' says Simon. 'Right, Julie?'

'This is all very sudden,' says Miss Elliot. 'Perhaps you should give us some time to think.'

Julie feels her temper rise. 'I'm sorry, I don't mean to be rude, but it's got nothing to do with you. I'm Helen's family; it's our business, not yours.'

'The school is acting as Helen's guardian —' Miss Elliot begins.

'But I'm her sister. I'm her next of kin!'

'Julie, slow down,' says Simon.

'She's my *sister*,' says Julie again. Impulsively she moves around the table and tries to embrace Helen. But Helen pushes her away. She has begun to cry. Sobbing, she starts to scrape together the scattered papers and shovel them back into the yellow envelope.

Julie says, 'What are you doing?'

'They're mine,' says Helen. 'Mine, not yours.'

Julie knows Helen is right, but she can't help feeling that the papers belong to her. She found them, they were Tony's. She scrabbles for the report cards, the letters, that Helen hasn't reached, clutching them to her chest.

'Julie . . .' says Simon.

The papers spill to the floor and both girls dive to

retrieve them. Their heads bang together, and Helen cries out. An arrow of pain shoots through Julie's skull, where she cut her head when she crashed the car that morning. Helen lets the papers fall, weeping bitterly, and Miss Elliot puts her arms around her. Julie, grimly determined, sweeps the papers into the envelope. She feels like crying too, but she won't let herself. This meeting has been such a mess; she has ruined everything. Her hands are shaking as she thrusts the last letter into the envelope and stands up.

'I think perhaps you should leave now,' says Miss Elliot.

Simon raises his hands placatingly. 'Okay. Okay.' He shoots a look at Julie, at the envelope in her hands. 'Maybe you should leave that here?'

Julie hugs the envelope to her chest; then she slowly lays it down on the table.

'Okay,' says Simon. He takes Julie's arm and steers her toward the door.

'Oh, please,' says Julie. 'Please —'

'Maybe we could come back tomorrow?' says Simon. 'Give us all a chance to cool down?' He looks at Miss Elliot, who hesitates, then gives an almost imperceptible nod of agreement.

Then Julie is stumbling down the stairs, with Simon gripping her elbow. Night is creeping through the streets;

the deafening thrum of cicadas rises from the garden. The sky is streaked with pink and orange like the lining of a passionfruit. Julie trips on the last step, and Simon catches her.

'Careful,' he says.

She tries to say *thanks*, but it bursts from her throat as a sob.

21

Safe inside the Jeep, Julie fishes a grubby handkerchief from the depths of her bag, scrubs at her eyes and takes a deep, shuddering breath. 'So,' she says. 'That didn't go very well, did it?'

'What did you expect?' says Simon, driving. 'Did you think she'd run into your arms and weep for joy?'

Julie says nothing. She stares out at the houses on stilts, nestled in their half-wild gardens. Not even colonial Goroka can tame the jungle completely.

'Sorry,' says Simon.

'Can we not talk about it?'

'It'll be better tomorrow,' says Simon. 'When she's had a chance to get used to the idea. You'll see.'

He steers the Jeep through the darkened streets of the town, searching for the motel Patrick recommended. They are too tired to speak. At last he pulls up outside a small, rundown motel. A faded sign announces *Paradise Lodge*. Simon switches off the engine.

'Finally,' he says.

Julie looks at him. 'Are you okay?'

'I've never driven this far before. Not the whole way.' He flexes his fingers. 'So.'

'I'm going to pay,' says Julie. 'I've got cash.'

'Don't book a room for me. I'll sleep in the Jeep.'

Julie hesitates, but she's too exhausted to argue with him. Anyway, should she be throwing money away on motel rooms? It might mean one more term at school for Helen. If Simon wants to sleep in the car, that's up to him. 'Fine,' she says wearily, and slips down from the Jeep.

She pushes open the door to reception. The stench of grease almost bowls her over. An elderly white man behind the counter is tucking into a plate of bacon, eggs and sausages, all slathered in tomato sauce. He peers up at her grumpily, not pleased to have his dinner interrupted.

'I'd like a room, please.'

The man looks past her shoulder for a companion that isn't there. 'On your own, are you?'

'Um — yes.'

'Bit young to be travelling alone, aren't you?'

Julie draws herself up. 'I'm eighteen,' she says. 'I've stayed by myself in hotels *hundreds* of times.'

'Oh, yeah?' He stares at her, sceptical. 'Single room?'

She hesitates only for a second. 'Double.' The temptation to stretch herself luxuriously in a huge bed after this longest of days is irresistible.

The manager gives her a leering look, and her heart sinks. 'Luggage?'

'It's in my car.'

'How many nights?'

She considers. 'Better make it two.'

He scratches himself. 'What are you doing in town, sweetheart?'

'Visiting family . . .' Why is she even answering his questions? She pulls out her purse. 'Can I pay now?'

He shrugs. 'If you want.'

Even as she's counting out the cash, she's berating herself. Dumb, dumb, you don't pay first! What if the room's no good? She's already given him the money; now she's got nothing to bargain with. But it's too late, she's too embarrassed to say she's changed her mind.

He pushes the register toward her and she signs it neatly. She *has* done this before, in Brisbane, before she flew up to Port Moresby. But Caroline booked that room. Julie only had to turn up and pay . . . She remembers, too late, that she meant to use a fake name — is that against the law? Oh, well, she's obviously not cut out for a life of crime.

The manager fishes a key from a hook and leads Julie outside, to a row of rooms whose doors face the car park. The Jeep is there, but she can't see Simon. Is he hiding? He wouldn't abandon her — would he?

The manager opens the door and stands aside so she can see the room. 'Very nice,' she says, distractedly. Is she supposed to tip him now, or something?

The man sniffs. 'You want some dinner? I could rustle you up some eggs or something. I can bring it to your room if you like. Maybe you'd like some company.' He leans against the doorjamb and looks her up and down.

'No, thanks.' She is repulsed, and she lets it show.

'Shit, I was just being friendly. No need to be a stuck-up little bitch.' He gives her a dirty look over his shoulder as he waddles away. Julie whisks inside and slams the door shut.

The room is clean. Clean-ish. A fluorescent tube flickers and buzzes. The double bed is covered with a crooked tartan rug. A drawing of a Highland warrior scowls down from one wall, a poster of a fluffy kitten is pinned to another. Julie wiggles the doorhandle. It seems very flimsy — She almost falls over as the door is pushed open.

It's Simon. He looks embarrassed but determined. 'I think I should sleep in here, on the floor. Just in case . . .

I saw the way that sleazy creep was looking at you; I don't trust him.'

Julie feels weak with relief. 'Yes, please. Please, do stay.'

They bring in the bags and food from the Jeep. Julie locks the door, and pushes a bedside table up against it for good measure. She switches on the reading lamp and turns off the harsh fluorescent light, and the room at once seems cosier, more friendly. Simon folds a rug from the car and sits on the floor, his back to the wall. 'What's for dinner?'

Julie investigates Dulcie's basket. She's been too nervous to eat all afternoon, but now suddenly she feels ravenous. 'Ham-and-cheese sandwiches. Tomatoes, bananas, hard-boiled eggs . . . Oh, and cake.'

'I feel as if I'm in the Famous Five,' says Simon.

For a moment Julie feels as if she's a little kid again, blessedly free from all her grown-up worries — Tony's death, Helen, Caroline's looming arrival, her own forced departure from New Guinea. It's as if they're playing cubbies in their own hidden den: cosy, safe and secret. She says, 'Your mother is *cool*.'

Simon is silent, unwrapping the greaseproof paper around the sandwiches. The soft light strikes his face so that the shadow of his eyelashes sweeps down his cheek. At last he says, 'It's taken me a while to appreciate her.'

Julie is quiet, waiting.

'I used to wish Dad had married a *normal* woman. A European woman. It really pissed me off. It made our lives so hard, you know? We'd go into town, people would cross to the other side of the street. And Mum's life, too. It's been harder for her.' He looks at Julie. 'It would be hard for Helen, too, you know. If she was parachuted into Australia. Not knowing anyone . . . It's such a different world. She's just a kid. It's a lot to ask.'

'Okay,' says Julie. '*Okay*, I get it.' She shreds the sandwich paper, not looking at Simon. 'I thought we were talking about your mother.'

'Yeah.' Simon sighs. 'She misses the village; she gets lonely, especially when I'm away at school. She never got to go past Grade Three; she can hardly write her name. It's not fair . . . She's smart; she could have done anything.'

'I thought you said it was the best of both worlds,' says Julie.

He smiles. 'The worst of both worlds, too.' His face splits in a giant yawn. 'Sorry. I've been up since six.'

'Oh, I didn't realise — sorry.' She watches as he shakes out the rug and spreads it on the threadbare carpet. 'You can't really sleep on the floor.'

'It's okay. It's not as hard as the beds at boarding school.'

'At least take a pillow.' She throws one down to him.

'Thanks.'

Julie reaches over and snaps off the lamp. Light leaks into the room around the edge of the skimpy curtains. She pulls the blankets over herself and lies on her back, staring at the ceiling. *Simon, there's plenty of room up here. I promise I won't —* No, no. She can't say that. *Simon, are you comfortable down there? Simon, this is ridiculous, isn't it? Come up on the bed.*

He is asleep. She can hear the deep, even rhythm of his breathing.

She is so tired, but she feels wide awake. She thinks about Helen.

This is not like paying the motel manager before she's seen the room. She has all the power in this situation; Helen has none. Perhaps she'll be able to persuade her to come to Australia, in spite of what Simon says. But what if she can't persuade her? Could she *make* her come?

This is uncomfortable knowledge. It makes Julie feel prickly and miserable. She doesn't want this power. She wants Helen to *want* to come with her. What was it Simon said? Run into her arms and weep for joy?

And how would you feel, she asks herself, *if someone turned up out of the blue and wanted to take you away from everything you knew? Think how much you hate it when your mum tries to force you into things you don't want to do. Now imagine it was a stranger.*

Julie grimaces into the darkness. She wanted this visit to be a wonderful meeting; but she's messed it up. Far below, sunk in the earth, she senses a slow, faint rumbling. It's a minor *guria*, too weak to shake the building; it's just strong enough to set up an uneasy quivering, rocking deep in her gut, like seasickness. Her hands creep out to hold onto the edge of the bed. Her eyes are wide open, staring into the dark.

*

'How did you sleep?'

Simon grimaces. 'Not very well. Terribly, actually.'

'Me either. I kept waking up and not knowing where I was.' Julie lets out a sigh as the Jeep rounds the corner and she sees that the green car is still parked underneath Miss Elliot's house. 'Oh, good. They're home.'

Simon glances at her. 'Did you think they'd run away?'

When he puts it like that, it sounds ridiculous; but some part of Julie had been afraid that she and Simon would arrive and find them gone.

Simon parks the Jeep, and once again they climb the steep steps. The front door opens almost before Julie has finished knocking.

'Come in,' says Miss Elliot.

The four of them stand awkwardly in the living room. Helen looks at the floor, her hands clasped in front of her. Today the clips in her hair are tiny birds.

Julie feels herself smiling nervously. Simon rubs the back of his head.

Miss Elliot says softly, 'Helen? Don't you have something to say?'

Helen keeps her eyes lowered. She murmurs, 'I'm sorry about yesterday. I was upset. But I shouldn't have behaved like that. It was rude and I apologise.'

This speech has obviously been carefully prepared. Julie can imagine Miss Elliot sitting Helen down and rehearsing it. Her stomach churns. This is all wrong. She, Julie, was the one who behaved like a spoilt brat yesterday — why would Miss Elliot make Helen apologise to her?

Miss Elliot shoots her a swift, worried, sideways glance, and in a flash Julie understands. It's because Julie is white, because she is rich, because she controls Tony's money now. This is horrible: to see Miss Elliot and Helen feeling forced to almost grovel to her, to stop her from abandoning Helen completely, so she isn't thrown out of the school . . . It shouldn't be like this. Julie is only offering what Helen is owed, what should be hers by right. Tony was her father, too. She is just as entitled to his inheritance as Julie is.

Julie flings out her hand. 'Don't! Please don't. I should be the one apologising. I shouldn't have snatched your reports and stuff. That was just — rude. I'm sorry. Can we — can we start again? Please?'

Miss Elliot and Helen look at each other. Then Miss Elliot turns to Simon. 'Perhaps you and I should go and sit in the kitchen? Would you like a coffee?'

Julie shakes her head.

'I'd love one,' says Simon, and he follows Miss Elliot into the kitchen. The door closes firmly behind them, and Julie feels a sudden unexpected twist of jealousy. What if Simon *fancies* Miss Elliot? She is shocked at how sick this thought makes her feel.

Helen and Julie are alone together.

Julie clears her throat. 'I really am sorry about yesterday.' There is a brief pause. 'I hope your head's okay.'

'No,' says Helen. 'I have a big lump. Here.' She touches her temple, and stares at Julie accusingly.

'Oh, God!' says Julie. 'Sorry!'

Helen puts her hand to her mouth and begins to giggle, and then Julie starts to giggle too.

'Let's sit down,' says Julie, and they settle side by side on the sagging brown couch.

Helen smoothes her hair, and Julie looks at her carefully. 'Your face is the same shape as Tony's. Your chin and your nose. I can see it.'

Helen nods. She says, 'Do you have a picture of him?'

'No.' Julie feels stricken. 'I'll get you one.'

'I never met him,' says Helen.

'I only met him a few weeks ago,' says Julie. 'He and my mum split up when I was three. Just before he came up here. Just before —' She takes a breath. 'Before you were born, I guess.'

Helen nods again. 'My mother has a husband now,' she says in a matter-of-fact tone. 'A new family.' She lowers her eyes and says softly, 'But it's better if I live here now.'

'Do you miss them?' says Julie. 'You must miss them.'

Helen shrugs. 'I do. But I can't live with them. They live far away. There's no school there. I have to go to school.' She shoots Julie a quick, intense look.

'I know,' says Julie. 'I know how important it is. I'll make sure you can keep going to school. Whatever happens. I promise.' She takes a deep breath. 'Look, it came out all wrong yesterday, but I meant what I said — if you wanted to, I'd really like you to come and live with us. With me and my mum. We live in Melbourne. It's a big city. We live near the sea, near the beach. You could go to my school . . .'

But Helen is shaking her head, gently but firmly. She says, 'I like my school. I want to stay at my school. I live with Miss Elliot in the holidays. She is like —' Helen bites back a word, then changes her mind, '— like a sister,' she finishes shyly.

Julie doesn't know what to say. 'That's — that's good. Good. It's good that — that you're happy.'

Helen nods. She seems relieved, as if a great danger has passed. 'I want to go to teachers' college one day,' she confides. 'Then I can be a teacher, like Miss Elliot. There is the teachers' college here in Goroka. Or perhaps I can go to the university in Port Moresby. Miss Elliot says I would be a good teacher, or a journalist for the newspapers, one day. We have our own newspaper, at school. We can put in stories. One of my stories was in the newspaper last term.'

Now it's Julie's turn to nod. 'That sounds great. You sound like you've got a better idea of what to do with your life than I do.'

Helen smiles, and tucks her hair behind her ear. She looks confident and self-possessed, and for a moment Julie envies her.

'If you change your mind about coming to Australia, just tell me, okay? I'll try to find a way to make it happen. But if you're sure you want to stay here, then I'll make sure your school fees get paid. After that —' She hesitates. 'I don't know, we'll have to see. I'll have to talk to my mother, and — there are other people

I can talk to.' She is thinking of Allan Crabtree, and Patrick and Dulcie. 'But I promise I'll do everything I can. Because we're family now.'

Helen nods. She holds out her hand, and Julie shakes it. Helen's hand is small and cool and dry.

'Maybe I could visit you in Australia, one day?' suggests Helen. Julie senses that she is suggesting it as a kindness to her, Julie.

'I would really like that,' says Julie. 'You could visit me and I could visit you.'

'I would like that, too,' says Helen.

Simon and Miss Elliot come out from the kitchen. Helen rises, and slips her hand into Miss Elliot's.

'It's all right,' she says. 'We've been talking. Julie says I can stay at the school. She will pay. It's all right. We're wontoks now.'

'That's right,' says Julie. 'We're wontoks.'

'Mr Murphy and I have been talking, too,' says Miss Elliot, and for a second Julie thinks that Patrick must somehow have magically arrived in Goroka while she and Helen have been sitting on the couch. 'If you're sure your family will take responsibility for Helen's education . . .' Miss Elliot glances at Simon. 'I wonder if perhaps you could set up a trust fund?'

'I can't be in charge of a trust fund,' says Julie. 'I'm not old enough.'

'I'm sure Allan Crabtree would be willing to be a trustee,' says Simon. 'And my dad would do it, I'm sure. And perhaps someone from the school?'

Miss Elliot nods. 'I will speak to our headmistress.'

Julie says to Simon, 'Couldn't you be one?'

Simon looks startled. 'I suppose so.'

'Please,' says Julie. 'Because I won't be here, you see.' She blinks, horrified, because there are tears in her eyes. She says, 'I wish I had a photo of you, Helen. To take home with me.'

Helen shoots a glance at Miss Elliot. Then she runs out of the room, and returns with the bulging yellow envelope. She rummages inside and pulls out the tiny black-and-white photograph. 'I have another copy of this one.' She holds it out to Julie. 'You can keep it.'

'Do you mean it? Thank you.' Julie folds her hand around the little photo, careful not to crease it. 'I just want to make sure you'll be okay. Even though Tony's gone. I want you to know you can rely on me.'

Helen lays her hand on Julie's arm. 'Please, don't worry about me. You don't need to rescue me. I'm all right.'

Julie looks at her half-sister. There are many things she wants to say to her. Helen is so young, but she is braver than Julie. Julie knows she could never have left home at twelve to go to school, and been so determined to stick to it, so clearly focused on the future. Julie wants to tell her she admires her; she wants to make her all kinds of promises.

But all she can bring herself to whisper is, 'Will you write to me?'

22

Miss Elliot takes a couple of photographs of Julie and Helen, in the garden. Julie and Simon eat lunch with them and then, politely but firmly, they are shown out into the early afternoon sunshine.

'Helen needs to rest now,' Miss Elliot says. 'She didn't sleep well last night.'

Julie can't help herself; she puts her arms around her sister and squeezes tight. 'Goodbye.'

'Goodbye.'

Julie holds onto the handrail as she descends the steps. The sun seems dazzling, the birds yelling in the trees. She says to Simon, 'What should we do now?'

Simon rubs his hand across his eyes. 'There's a park we could walk in, I think — or — listen, would you mind if we went back to the motel? I think I need an afternoon nap too.'

'I wouldn't mind.'

Back at the Paradise Lodge, the bed has been made, Simon's pillow replaced and his rug neatly folded. For some reason this makes Julie feel embarrassed. She pulls the curtains closed and kicks off her shoes. Without speaking, without discussing it, they lie down on the bed, side by side. The springs creak and sag; they are not touching, but Simon's body is so close to hers she can feel the warmth radiating from his skin.

Julie gazes up at the ceiling. Damp stains have traced a map on the fibro sheeting: hills and valleys, lakes and islands. A whole foreign country, drawn on the sky.

'You should be prepared,' says Simon. 'Some people are going to give you a hard time over this.'

'Over what?'

'Signing away Tony's money to a half-caste bastard.' She hears his head shift on the pillow as he turns to glance at her. 'That's what they're going to say, Julie.'

'Who's going to say that?'

'Maybe your mother. People like the Crabtrees. Most expats. They're going to think you're a sentimental idiot.'

'I don't care what they think,' she says. 'It's the right thing to do. She was his daughter, too.'

'Yes.' There is a pause. 'Just be prepared, that's all I'm saying.'

'I am.'

'Good.'

There is another silence. The room is warm and shadowy. Outside, a bird's call rings out, echoes and dies away.

'Helen told me she wants to be a teacher,' Julie says. 'Or a journalist.'

'I can imagine that. She seems as if she'd keep her cool, doesn't she?' says Simon. 'So that's her future all planned out . . . what are we going to do with you?'

Julie sighs. 'I'm *supposed* to be a lawyer. That's what Caroline wants me to do. Become a lawyer and fight for Women's Lib. Or human rights, or legal aid, or something.'

'You don't sound particularly enthusiastic.'

'That's not what I want. I'm sure about that now. I want to stay here, in New Guinea.'

'Plenty of work for lawyers up here,' says Simon. 'Those raskols we met on the road. The guy who broke into your house. Even Helen. They could all do with a good lawyer.'

'But I don't think I'd be a good lawyer,' says Julie. 'That's the point.'

'So what do you want to do?'

'I don't know.'

He is quiet for a moment, then he says, 'You know, if you're serious about wanting to be an administrator, there are things you could do. You could learn book-keeping, for a start. Then *anyone* would give you a job.

There are probably courses you could do. You should find out.'

'Mm.' She knows he's right. What he says makes sense. But she's impatient. She doesn't want to slog through a university course or a training college. She wants to be here now.

Simon is saying, 'I'm sure we could find something for you to do. If you do come back.'

'I don't have to come back,' she says. 'If I never leave.'

Simon shifts beside her. 'What do you mean?'

'Well, what if — what if I stayed here? I could go to Wewak or Madang, and get a job waitressing at one of the hotels, and then I could visit Helen sometimes.'

A kind of snort escapes from Simon. 'You think dropping out of school is a good idea? And what would your mother say to that?'

'I wouldn't have to tell her where I was. If I went now — today, or tomorrow — before she gets here, she'd never find me. I'd ring her,' she adds quickly. 'And tell her I was okay. Obviously. I wouldn't want her to worry.'

Simon shifts onto his side. It's dim in the room with the curtains shut, and Julie feels, rather than sees, his eyes searching her face. He says, 'You can't be serious.'

'Why not?' Her voice rises in a defensive squeak. 'Places like that always need waitresses. Or I could clean rooms . . .'

'Julie, those jobs pay nothing. They're *kanaka* jobs.'

She won't let him shock her. 'Then I'll get an office job. I'm good at that. I can type. Allan Crabtree said he'd give me a job. I'll tell them I'm eighteen. I did that last night, the manager believed me.'

Simon groans. 'This is a crazy idea. It's not a plan. You don't have a visa, remember?'

'I'll get a job first, then they'll have to give me a visa.'

'It doesn't work like that . . . And they'd find you in ten seconds flat and ship you home so fast your feet wouldn't touch the ground. And they'd *never* let you come back again. And that —' his voice drops to a whisper, '— that would be a bloody shame.'

Julie swallows hard. It's a moment before she can speak, and when she does, her voice is wobbly. 'I don't want to go home. I want to stay here.'

'Everyone has to leave, Julie. I had to leave, too. You'll find a way to come back, if you really want to.' His voice is gentle and sad.

'Coming to New Guinea — it's made me feel like —' She pauses. 'You know when you're flying, and it's all clouds below, and you can't see anything? And then all of a sudden the clouds are gone, and you can see the whole country spread out beneath you. Mountains and valleys and trees and houses — a whole world, and it was there all the time, and you never realised. As if anything was possible . . .'

She rolls onto her side, facing him. She feels the stir of his breath against her lips and her cheeks, lifting a strand of her hair. There is a hand's breadth between their bodies; she can almost feel the crackle of lightning as it leaps across the gap. She never felt like this when she was close to Ryan. Ryan would crowd too close, suffocating her, so that she'd have to pull away, so she could breathe again. But here, now, with Simon, she longs to move closer. She wants to touch him, to touch his smooth skin and run her hands over the planes of his body. She wants to inhale the scent of him, merge her breath with his.

She lifts her head, the slightest movement. He is watching her; his eyes are dark and huge, his brow faintly creased. He murmurs her name; it might be a question, or a plea. She whispers, 'Ssh.' She feels giddy, but also very sure of herself as she leans forward and touches her lips to his.

He lets his fingers brush against her back, then pulls them away. She is the one who unbuttons his shirt, who slides her hands down the sides of his body, who presses herself against his warm chest and his wildly beating heart.

He kisses her tentatively; when he touches her, it's as if he's exploring a new land, step by hesitant step. She laces her fingers through his and holds on tight; they've come so far, she's not about to let him lose his way now.

23

The hammering at the door comes as an explosion. Julie is stunned awake, gasping. Simon's arms had been wrapped around her, but now he tears himself free, throwing himself off the bed, scrabbling for his clothes.

The angle of the light has shifted; they must been asleep for a couple of hours at least. It's late afternoon.

The banging at the door intensifies. Confusedly she assumes it's the raskol gang, come to seize her roll of cash. 'What do we do? They're going to bash the door down!'

Simon hitches up his jeans and peers through the crack in the curtains. He says, unnaturally calm, 'It's Allan and Ryan Crabtree. Do you want to let them in?'

'No,' says Julie. 'Not really.'

'Julie! Julie! We know you're in there!' shouts Ryan. The door rattles violently. 'Are you okay?'

'Yes!' yells Julie. She swings her legs over the side of the bed, quickly buttons up her shirt and yanks at her skirt to straighten it up. Simon is hauling on his shirt. She says, 'I'd better let them in.'

Simon half-shrugs and turns away as Julie fumbles with the lock. As the door begins to open, Ryan and Allan almost fall inside the room. The sudden light from the doorway reveals Julie and Simon, rumpled, but fully dressed; Ryan, panting and furious, his fists clenched and raised; and Allan, scowling, his eyes narrowed and darting around the room. With a violent movement, he drags the curtains open, and the watery afternoon light wavers in. The double bed, with its ravaged landscape of crumpled blankets, stands like an accusation.

'What the hell is going on?' shouts Ryan. 'What have you done to her, you little prick?'

'*What?* What are you talking about?' Julie steps back.

Ryan barely glances at her. 'You are in so much trouble,' he says to Simon. 'In a hotel room with a white girl —'

'Settle down!' barks Allan. He looks at Julie. 'Are you all right, love? He hasn't hurt you?'

'*Yes*, I'm all right. Of course he hasn't —'

'What's that?' Ryan springs forward, pointing triumphantly to the matted clump of hair above Julie's ear.

Julie gingerly touches her head. 'I banged my head —' Perhaps she shouldn't mention crashing Tony's car. 'It was an accident,' she says lamely.

'It's okay, love, it's over now. We've found you; we've come to take you home.' Allan approaches, his arm outstretched to embrace her, but Julie backs away.

'But I don't want to come home — What are you *doing* here?'

'— looking for you all over town —'

'— Teddie Spargo —'

'— Patrick Murphy shut up like a clam —'

They are all speaking at once; all except Simon, who stands silently in the corner of the room. Then suddenly, as if at a signal, everyone falls quiet.

'Don't feel like you have to protect him,' says Ryan. 'Just say the word and I'll give him a smack in the mouth.'

'Shut up!' roars Allan, his face bright red. He turns to Julie. 'Tell me straight, love. Did he force you to come with him?'

'*No!*' Julie actually stamps her foot. 'If anything, *I* forced *him*. He didn't want me to drive to Goroka on my own . . .'

'Why the hell did you want to come to Goroka?' says Ryan.

'I was looking for —' Julie stops. 'I was looking for my half-sister.'

'*What?*' Ryan bursts into laughter, until a glare from Allan shuts him up.

'When I was clearing out Tony's flat —' *God, could that be only yesterday?* '— I found some papers. He has another daughter; she's at school here. Her name's

Helen. Here, look.' She fumbles in her bag for the little photo and thrusts it into Allan's hands.

Ryan whistles. 'Mac had a dirty little accident? Jeez, he managed to keep that quiet.'

'Shut up!' says Julie fiercely. 'That's my sister you're talking about.'

Allan is frowning over the photograph. 'You are sure about this, love? Some native girl might have tried to tie one on; it does happen.'

Julie tries to stay calm. 'You didn't know about Helen?'

'Not a bloody word.'

'It's true. He gave her his surname; he's been paying her school fees all this time. And she — she looks like him.'

'So you found her then?' Allan looks up sharply. 'What about the mother?'

'Helen told us she's married; she's got a new family. Helen wants to stay at the school, if she can. She's happy there, she's doing well.'

Allan passes a hand over his face. He says slowly, 'There was that girl, the meri, when Mac first came up here . . . He said she ran off back home. Didn't think any more about it at the time.'

Ryan reaches eagerly for the photo, shaking his head. 'The dirty dog!'

Wildly, Julie swings her fist into his face. There is a crunch of bone on bone. Ryan leaps backward, yelping, and clutches at his nose. Blood streams between his fingers. 'Shit!'

Julie sees Simon turn away to hide a smile. 'Sorry —' she says. 'I didn't mean to —' Her hand stings, but she's determined not to show it.

Ryan stumbles toward the tiny bathroom. He emerges a moment later, trailing streamers of bloodied toilet paper, his hands pressed to his face. He stares accusingly at Julie, then at his father. 'Did you see that?' he demands.

Allan is unmoved. 'You had it coming.' He gathers up the papers and stuffs them back into the envelope. 'Okay. I can see why you went rushing off. But you should have told us what was going on.'

'I couldn't wait,' mumbles Julie. 'I left a message with Teddie. I needed to see Helen — to tell her —'

Allan breaks in. 'Your mother's here.'

'*Here?*' Incredulous, Julie cranes past him.

'In Hagen. She arrived this morning. Not keeping people informed of your movements runs in the family, apparently. She nearly went berserk when we couldn't track you down. That's why we're here. She's come to take you home.'

Julie sits down on the end of the bed. 'Oh.'

Alan consults his heavy, complicated airman's watch. 'We've got time to make it if we leave now. The clouds have cleared.'

'You flew here?'

'Of course,' says Ryan, muffled by wads of toilet paper.

Julie shoots Simon a quick, anxious glance. 'I'd rather drive back with Simon tomorrow . . .'

Ryan snorts. 'Yeah, I'll bet. You reckon we'd let you stay another night?'

Allan says briskly, 'Driving back will take too long. Your mum wants to see you ASAP.'

Simon says, 'I can't drive back today. I'm bushed, I need some sleep.'

'So you didn't get any last night, then?' jeers Ryan. 'Sleep, I mean —'

Allan rounds on him. 'Do you want a smack from me as well? Go and wait for us outside.'

Ryan's mouth falls open. 'But —'

'Get out!' bellows Allan.

Silently Ryan pulls open the door and sulks outside.

'We didn't,' says Julie. 'Me and Simon, we didn't —'

Allan holds up a hand to stop her. 'I don't want to know. Come on, love, get your things together.'

Julie picks up her shoulder bag, and shuffles her feet into her shoes. She looks helplessly at Simon. 'The room's paid for. You can stay here tonight.'

He nods his head.

'Thanks — for coming with me,' she says.

He smiles. 'No worries.'

'Wrap it up, love,' says Allan. 'Time to say goodbye.'

Simon holds out his hand for her to shake, and it's not until that instant that Julie understands that this is really goodbye, that she may not see him again, that this could actually be the final moment. She doesn't want to shake his hand; she doesn't want to say goodbye that way. But she can't, she can't kiss him with Allan standing there.

She takes his hand and whispers, 'Goodbye, Simon.'

He holds her hand without shaking it; he holds it in his. His eyes are dark and bright. 'Goodbye, Julie.'

Allan clears his throat. 'You've got one minute,' he growls, and bangs the door behind him.

*

Goroka airport in is the middle of town. Julie sits on a plastic chair. It feels strange to be on the passenger's side of the waiting room instead of bustling about behind the counter. She clasps her shoulder bag on her lap. Her fingernails dig into her arms, carving tiny moons into her flesh. Ryan has gone for a walk; he's pacing up and down under the covered walkway outside.

Allan comes back. He says, 'We've got a slot in half an hour.'

Julie looks up at him blankly.

Allan sits down beside her. For a moment he says nothing, then he clears his throat and says gruffly, 'I'll keep an eye on the little girl for you.'

Julie rubs her eyes with the heels of her hands. She says, haltingly, 'Simon suggested something about a trust — maybe you and Patrick Murphy and he could be in charge of it — and the head of Helen's school? Or Helen's mother? I don't know how that stuff works.'

She wishes she could take charge of all this herself. It occurs to her that, before she came to New Guinea, it would never have crossed her mind to *want* to take charge.

'Don't worry about it,' says Allan. 'I'll send you quarterly reports, how about that? We'll manage.' He drops his meaty hand onto her shoulder. 'I promise.'

'I just wish —' She gives up trying to pretend that she isn't crying. 'I wish I could stay. I don't want to go back down south.'

'Yeah, well,' says Allan grimly. 'You and me both, kiddo.'

Julie gulps and wipes her eyes on her sleeve. 'Barbara wants to go back to Australia, doesn't she?'

'She is going,' says Allan. 'And the kids. And probably the bloody dog while they're at it.'

Julie stares at him. 'But — you're not?'

'There's nothing back there for me.' He gazes out at the Goroka airstrip, with its backdrop of mountains and high, rolling cloud. He says, 'My whole life is up here. If I go down south, I may as well shoot myself.'

Julie stares out through the glass. From the corner of her eye, she can see Ryan, marching moodily up and down, his head lowered, kicking at pebbles. She wonders why he and Nadine and Barbara don't count as being part of Allan's *whole life*. Her heart feels hollowed out, as fragile as a blown eggshell.

Allan says abruptly, 'Don't mention it to the kids, eh? We haven't told them yet.'

'So — does that mean you and Barbara will be getting divorced?'

Allan lifts his shoulders and lets them drop. He sits with his hands clasped between his knees. His face looks grey and old and hopeless.

Julie picks up his hand. He looks down at her, startled, but she doesn't let go, and they sit there, staring out at the pale sky, waiting until it's time to fly.

24

It's almost dark. Julie leans her head against the car window and gazes up at the interlaced branches of hibiscus that weave a perforated canopy over the Crabtrees' driveway.

Allan stops the car.

'Julie! Julie!'

Her mother is running to meet her, sweeping her into a hug. Julie stumbles against her, shocked. Caroline hardly ever hugs her . . . But Julie can't help clinging to her, to her familiar mum smell, and tears spring to her eyes.

'Oh, darling,' says Caroline, holding her tightly. 'This is such an awful thing to happen to you — to lose your father —'

Julie pulls herself away. She says, 'It didn't happen to me. It happened to Tony.'

'Well, yes, but —' Caroline frowns, then smiles uncertainly. She puts up a tentative hand and brushes back Julie's hair. 'You look different. You've got a tan.'

'Sorry,' Julie says. 'I'm — really tired.'

Caroline drops her hand. 'Of course. Of course you are.'

'Hot bath for you, I think,' says Barbara briskly. 'And then bed.' She puts her arm around Julie and leads her into the house. Behind them, Julie can hear Caroline's anxious, questioning voice, and the low, impatient growl of Allan's answers. A car door slams, more violently than necessary — that must be Ryan.

She bolts the bathroom door and slides into the warm bath, all the way down so that the water closes over her ears. All the voices, all the noises of the house — Roxy barking, Ryan stomping around in the kitchen on the hunt for food, calling to Koki, the thumping of the stereo, Nadine's shrill singing — it all merges into an indistinct hum, and she doesn't have to listen any more.

*

Caroline knocks, but doesn't wait for an answer before she pokes her head around the bedroom door. 'I've brought you a Milo.'

'Oh. Thanks.'

'There's no proper milk, I'm afraid.'

'That's okay, I'm used to it now. I like it.'

Caroline perches on the other bed while Julie sips, more from politeness than because she really wants the drink. The smell of the warm milk makes her feel slightly sick. After a pause, her mother says, 'Would you like me to brush your hair?'

Julie can't help pulling a face. 'You haven't done that since I was ten!'

'Maybe I could read to you for a while?'

'I haven't got a book . . .'

'Okay.' Another pause. 'Is there anything you'd like to talk about, darling?'

Julie sets down her mug on the bedside table and tries to smile. 'Maybe later? I'm pretty tired. I think I'd just like to go to sleep now.'

'All right.'

But Caroline lingers, sitting on the bed. She says, 'This really is an extraordinary place, isn't it? The people are so poor, there's so much need. I had no idea . . . and it's so close by. I was really shocked. The conditions, the dirt, the disease . . . All those poor little children . . .'

Julie thinks of the kids *gumi*-ing down the river in rubber tyres, shrieking with delight. She thinks of Miss Elliot and Helen, and kind, capable Dulcie. She thinks of dependable Koki and strong Moses and canny, shrewd Joseph from the HAC terminal. She remembers the raskols, with machetes in their belts, and the burglar who casually strolled away. She thinks of the bustle of the market, and the deep peace of the bush. But she can't find the words to convey all this to Caroline.

She says, 'There's more to it than that, Mum. It's beautiful, too.'

'Well, yes, I suppose so,' says Caroline. 'But you shouldn't romanticise a place just because it has a beautiful landscape. You have to look beyond the physical beauty; you have to see past the picturesque. That's a typical colonial reaction . . .'

'You only just got here! You don't know anything about it! You're not an expert on everything, you know —' A pause. 'Sorry, Mum.'

'You're tired,' says Caroline. 'It's all right. We can talk in the morning.'

She leans across awkwardly to kiss Julie's cheek. Julie lies stiffly, her arms by her sides.

'Good night, darling.'

'Night.'

Caroline snaps off the light, and tiptoes out of the room. Julie lies on her back, gazing at the roof. She can hear the words coming out of her own mouth, when she speaks to her mother: *being difficult*. She doesn't want to be mean to her, but it's as if she can't help resisting. She doesn't want to be Caroline's daughter again, not yet, not here. Not in this place where she is Tony's daughter, even now that Tony has gone.

Nadine's poster of a horse's head looms over her, staring down with huge, liquid eyes. Murmuring voices float down the corridor from the living room; she strains to make out what they're saying, but she can't hear. The music has stopped.

There is a tap at the door. 'It's me,' hisses Nadine. 'Can I come in?'

'It's your room.' Julie sits up.

Nadine bounds onto the bed. 'Jeez, Ryan's really pissed off with you,' she announces cheerfully. 'What happened to his nose? Did Simon Murphy punch him?'

'No, I did,' says Julie.

Nadine slaps her hands over her mouth to muffle a crow of laughter; snorts and snuffles escape between her fingers. After a moment Julie gives a reluctant giggle. She says weakly, 'It's not funny.'

She is very conscious of knowing something that Nadine doesn't know; that the family is breaking apart, that this will be her last summer in New Guinea. The knowledge sits like an iron weight between them on the bed.

'Do you want Roxy to sleep on your bed tonight?'

Julie is touched. 'No, that's okay. But thanks.'

Nadine wriggles closer, and lowers her voice. 'Is it true what they're talking about? That Tony had a native kid?'

'Are they talking about it?' Julie struggles out from beneath the blankets. 'What are they saying?'

'Don't bother going out there,' says Nadine. 'As soon as you turn up they'll stop talking.'

Julie recognises the truth of this. She lies down again, tormented.

Nadine hugs her knees. 'I could sing to you, if you like,' she says. 'When I was a kid and I couldn't sleep, sometimes Koki would sing to me.'

'Thanks,' says Julie. 'I'd like that.'

She closes her eyes, and Nadine croons to her in Pidgin. After a few minutes she breaks off. 'Sorry,' she says. 'I've forgotten some of the words.'

'I don't mind,' murmurs Julie.

So Nadine sings again, her voice hardly louder than a whisper, until Julie falls asleep.

*

'They are trying to move the natives — the nationals —' Barbara corrects herself quickly, '— out of those awful huts. There's a huge building program going on. But in a few years time, they'll be slums, I expect.'

'Oh, surely not,' says Caroline. 'If you give people decent places to live, they take pride in looking after them.'

Barbara gives a sceptical sniff. 'Maybe you're right . . . I won't be here to see it, anyway, thank God.'

'Oh, you're leaving?'

'Yes. Well . . .' Barbara shoots Julie a sideways look. 'We're not sure yet. We're still deciding what to do. It all depends if people like us will still be welcome here, after Independence.'

Still deciding? thinks Julie. *Huh.*

'Eat up, darling,' says Caroline. 'You look peaky.'

Julie pokes listlessly at her egg. The smell of bacon reminds her so strongly of the motel in Goroka that she feels as if she's going to choke. She mumbles, 'I'm not that hungry.'

'We should take you to the market, while you're here,' Barbara says brightly. 'It would be a shame for you to come all this way and not do some sightseeing.'

'We could go out to Keriga,' says Julie. 'So Caroline can see where Tony's buried.'

'I don't think we'll have time, will we?' says Caroline.

Julie pushes on doggedly. 'And we need to talk to Patrick Murphy. About setting up the trust for Helen.'

Caroline and Barbara exchange a swift glance. 'Well,' says Caroline. 'We don't want to rush into anything, darling.'

'But her school fees for next term will be due soon.'

'There's plenty of time to talk about it, once we get back to Melbourne.'

'But —'

'Julie,' says Caroline. 'Of course we want to do what's best for this girl, but we need to be sensible. I don't want you to regret anything. You know I'm not

263

rich, sadly. This money of Tony's might be the only bit of extra help you'll ever get. We need to think about it carefully . . .'

'I don't want to wait,' says Julie. 'I want to sort it out now.'

Caroline spreads her hands flat on the tabletop. 'I love you, darling. I want what's best for you. I know I haven't always made the right decisions —'

Julie looks up in horror to see tears in her mother's eyes.

'— I should have encouraged you and Tony to meet sooner, I'm sorry about that. I was trying to protect you, I suppose. But I'm worried about your future. What if you need that money, what if something happens?'

'You can't stop bad things happening,' says Julie. 'No one can. What about Tony?'

Caroline looks at the table. 'Yes,' she says. 'Life is short, isn't it?'

There is a silence. Julie waits. She knows she is going to win this battle.

At last Caroline looks up. 'All right,' she says. 'Let's find out what we need to do.'

25

The Crabtrees' telephone is in the kitchen, which means that all phone calls are more or less public. Julie waits until everyone is sitting out on the verandah after lunch on Sunday, then she slips away as if she were going to the bathroom. Koki turns around from the sink and gives her a friendly smile. Julie smiles back as she gingerly eases the door shut and takes the phone to the limit of its cord, into the corner of the room. She sits on the floor and dials the number for Keriga.

The phone seems to ring for a long time before someone picks it up. 'Hello?'

'Dulcie, is that you? This is Julie.'

There is a brief pause. 'Hello.'

Suddenly Julie doesn't know what to say. A mysterious lump has hardened in her throat. 'Could — could I please speak to Simon?'

'He's not here. He's coming back tomorrow.'

'But I'm leaving tomorrow!'

'He got some jobs to do in Goroka. Some shopping, you know. Business work.'

'Okay,' says Julie helplessly.

'You find your *susa*, that's good, *ya*?'

'Yes. I'm so happy we found her.'

There is another pause. 'Simon ring us; he tell us what happen.'

'I'm sorry,' whispers Julie.

'What for?' says Dulcie, in her matter-of-fact way. 'Not your fault.'

Julie winds the coils of the phone cord round her finger and lets them spring away. 'Dulcie? Would you give Simon a message from me?'

'Mm?'

'Would you tell him — tell him to write to me?'

Dulcie chuckles. 'No need to tell him that.'

'This is my address — will you give it to him?' Julie begins to dictate, but Dulcie stops her.

'You wait — my writing not so good. I get Mr Murphy.'

'Oh! I didn't think — sorry!' But Dulcie has already put the phone down. A few moments later, Julie hears Patrick's gruff voice.

'Yes, hello? You still here, are you? We all thought you must have left town already.'

'Tomorrow,' says Julie. 'Please, could you give Simon my address?'

'Fire away.'

Julie dictates her address and waits while Patrick writes it down; then she carefully copies down the Murphys' post office box number. 'And tell him, if he's ever in Melbourne . . .' Her voice trails away.

There is a silence. Julie can hear Patrick's wheezing breath. She knows Simon won't be coming to Melbourne. She says, 'Allan Crabtree is going to call you. About setting up the trust for Helen.'

'Ah, Simon mentioned something about that. Glad you're going to do the right thing by the little girl.'

'Well, we're going to try.' She leans her head against the wall. She says, 'Our flight to Moresby is at twelve o'clock tomorrow. If — if Simon comes home in time —'

'He thought you'd already gone,' says Patrick. 'I'll tell him. He likes you, you know.'

Julie swallows. 'I like him, too.'

*

On the final morning, Julie's bags are packed, the carved head wedged inside her suitcase, Tony's Pidgin phrasebooks in a paper carrier bag under her arm.

'What are all those books, sweetheart? Are you going to take them on the plane?'

'I want to start learning as soon as I can.'

'Oh, darling,' says Caroline. 'Don't you have enough to study at school?'

'I'll need it,' says Julie. She takes a deep breath. 'When I come back.' She adds cunningly, 'You said yourself, there's so much to do here. Especially for women . . . I might be able to help. They're setting up a whole new country, you know.'

Caroline opens her mouth and closes it again. She gives Julie a long look, and suddenly Julie is sure that her mother can see right through her.

'And I thought maybe I should learn bookkeeping.'

Unwillingly Caroline smiles. 'Well, if you've got your heart set on it . . . I suppose I could help you find a good course, after you finish school. If you're sure that's what you want.'

'I'm sure,' says Julie. Impulsively she throws her arms around her mother and kisses her cheek.

Caroline wraps her arms around her daughter, and they rock gently in a silent embrace.

Julie props the carrier bag against her suitcase, by the front door. The fish hook that Tony talked about has lodged in her heart, and she knows that as long as she lives, New Guinea will keep tugging at her. But she also knows that, no matter how confidently she assures Caroline that she's coming back, part of her is waiting for a sign. Waiting for Simon.

Barbara is driving them to the airport. Julie paces the living room, listening out for the sound of a

Jeep crunching down the driveway. But there is nothing.

Caroline says, 'Ryan? Are you coming to see us off?'

Ryan shrugs. 'Nads wants to go. I won't fit in the car.'

Since they've returned from Goroka, he's refused to speak to Julie, though nobody but Nadine seems to have noticed this. Barbara would pointedly leave them alone together, whereupon Ryan would walk out of the room, much to Julie's relief.

'I'm sure the three of us could squeeze into the back,' says Caroline helpfully.

Ryan scowls. Without answering, he picks up his guitar and stalks out onto the verandah. He throws himself into the swinging chair and begins to strum some melancholy chords, staring out across the misty valley. Julie follows him outside.

'Ryan.'

He frowns down at the frets of his guitar.

'Ryan, I'm sorry about . . .' she wants to say *your nose*, but she changes it to, '. . . the way everything worked out.'

'You should have told me.' He still won't look at her. 'If you liked him better than me. You should have said something.'

'I know. I'm sorry.' Julie swallows. 'I was trying to be —'

'You know what? It doesn't matter.' At last he looks up, angry green light flickering in his eyes. 'Forget about it.'

'I don't want things to end like this,' says Julie. She feels as if she's reciting lines from a movie. This scene feels artificial, staged, but Ryan's feelings are real. She has hurt him. She didn't mean to, but she has. 'Can't we still be friends?'

'No,' says Ryan. 'I don't think so.'

He bends his head and strums at his guitar. After a moment, Julie says, 'Thanks for looking after me. When Dad died.'

He doesn't look up, but one shoulder twitches in a shrug.

She watches him for a minute longer. She supposes she should feel sad, but what she actually feels is mostly relief. She turns on her heel and walks back inside the house.

When she and her mother and Barbara and Nadine, all pile into the car an hour later, Ryan doesn't come out to wave goodbye.

'He's a very sensitive boy,' Barbara murmurs to Caroline as they head to the airport. 'He hates goodbyes.' She lowers her voice so that Julie can barely hear her. 'First love . . . so difficult.'

Caroline twists around to throw a startled look at her daughter. Julie glares out of the window and pretends

270

not to notice. Nadine nudges her, and makes a gagging gesture.

'Don't worry; he'll get over it,' she whispers. 'Last summer he was in love with Lynette Spitelli.'

Julie nods, and turns her attention back to the window. The road to the airport has become a familiar landscape — they drive past the police barracks, down and up the dip in the road where the white line wobbles comically, past the Chinese trade store and the A-frame house. Time is running out.

And then they're there.

She cranes out of the window, but she sees at once that there is no Jeep waiting in the car park. That was it, the last chance; it's too late.

The smell of the terminal, coffee beans and cats, must and sweat, rises around her like a mist. Teddie rushes out of the office and envelops Julie in a vanilla-scented hug.

'I'll write to you,' she whispers in Julie's ear. 'And I wanted you to be the first to know. We're going to have a baby!'

Julie hugs her. She knows she should be thrilled, or at least that she should act as if she is; but she is struggling to feel anything at all. She has the sense that she's trapped in a kind of dream which will play out without any assistance from her, rolling on to its conclusion whether she is there or not. In a few minutes they will be on the plane; soon she will be gone, a vanishing speck, spiralling into the sky, disappearing as if she'd never been here at all.

Now Joseph is weighing their bags on the big scales; now Allan comes marching toward them with his pilot's cap pushed to the back of his head. And then, all too soon, Barbara and Nadine are hugging her, and she is walking, dazed, out onto the tarmac, following Caroline across to the plane. She is climbing inside. This is it, the final moment. She says to Allan, 'Can I sit up front?'

'Don't you want to sit with your mother?' says Caroline in mock — or genuine — hurt.

'I can see better from here,' says Julie. 'Please, Mum. It might be my last chance for a while.'

Caroline nods. 'All right, darling. I understand.'

Then it's the smell of the upholstery and the shadowy odour of all the human bodies and all the cargo that has shifted in and out of the balus. Julie buckles her seatbelt and twists to stare out of the window, for her last look at the mountains, and the painted cloud backdrop of the Highland sky. Allan slams his door and starts up the engines.

Suddenly Julie grabs his arm. 'Wait! Wait!' she shouts, and points to where Nadine is racing across the tarmac toward the plane.

'Shit!' yells Allan. 'What the hell is she playing at?' He switches the engines off, the propellers hum and slow down and stop. Allan flings open his door. 'You bloody little idiot! Do you know how dangerous —'

'Sorry, sorry, Dad,' pants Nadine. 'I just had to give Julie this. He said she'd know what it meant.'

She hands up an envelope through the doorway, spins around and sprints back to the terminal building.

'Jesus!' Allan bangs the door shut again. He tosses the envelope onto Julie's lap. 'What the hell was all that about?' Scowling, he restarts the engines and the propellers whir into life once more.

Julie presses her face to the window. In the HAC car park, a battered Jeep is pulled up at an angle which suggests the driver screeched up in a hurry, the front door flung open. On the narrow grassy slope between the car park and the asphalt, a figure stands, staring anxiously toward the plane. Julie raises her hand; she waves frantically. He has to see her —

Nadine is on the grass, jumping up and down. Allan had stopped the plane for her; he wouldn't have stopped for Simon.

The figure raises one hand — not waving — it's a salute. The plane begins to taxi forward, swinging toward the runway, carrying her away.

Desperately, Julie rips open the envelope. There is no letter inside, no note, no card. She draws out a single slender feather, a lacy feather, tipped with a blue-and-white eye, like a peacock's tail.

A sob tears at Julie's throat. She presses both hands against the perspex of the window, her eyes locked on the figure on the grass, drawing further and further away with every second. 'Yes!' she shouts. 'Yes, yes!' She nods vigorously. Half-laughing, half-crying, she blinks away tears. The plane's engines rev and roar, and now they are racing along the runway. The figure stands on the grass, as motionless as the mountains. And now the plane is lifting into the sky, and the figure is dwindling smaller and smaller, but he is still there, gazing steadily into the clouds, as if nothing could ever move him, as if he would always be there.

Caroline leans forward between the seats. 'What's that, darling?' she shouts above the drone of the engines. 'What's going on?'

'Nothing,' Julie yells back. 'It's a feather from a Victoria Crowned pigeon.' She holds it up to show her mother. 'They're very intelligent birds,' she shouts. 'Very faithful.'

She turns away from her mother's puzzled face, and touches the tip of the feather gently to her lips. Below them, the clouds are drifting, as noiseless as a dream; and the mountains are waiting.

But Julie's head is full of the image of Simon, standing there, staring upward.

And this is one of the pictures that will come into Julie's mind in the months to come. Every time she looks at the feather, every time she touches it with her lips, morning and night; and when she sees the Independence parades on the television news, and pins one of the new nation's flags to her bedroom wall, with its stars and its bird of paradise; whenever she creases open one of Tony's phrasebooks to memorise another few words of Pidgin; and every time she deposits her weekend waitressing pay into her bank account: she will think of him, standing on the verandah at Keriga; and of Helen, her head bent over her books in a classroom in Goroka; and of Tony's grave, in the sunlit valley, under the waving grass; and of the planes trundling over the tarmac to the HAC terminal.

And whenever she looks up at the silver circle of the moon, she will knows that the same moon is shining down on New Guinea, and she will hope that Simon is looking up at it, too, and thinking of her.

And she dreams, and works, and saves, and waits, for the day when he will be standing by the side of the airstrip, on the day she returns, when the plane spirals down, bringing her home.

About the author

Kate Constable is a Melbourne writer who grew up in Papua New Guinea, where her father worked as a charter pilot. She is the author of the internationally-published fantasy trilogy, The Chanters of Tremaris, as well as *The Taste of Lightning*. As part of the *Girlfriend* fiction series she wrote *Always Mackenzie* and *Winter of Grace* (joint winner of the Children's Peace Literature Award, 2009) and co-authored *Dear Swoosie* (with Penni Russon). Her novel *Cicada Summer* was short-listed for the 2010 Prime Minister's Literary Award.

Her most recent novel, *Crow Country*, won the 2012 Children's Book Council of Australia Book of the Year Award (younger readers) and the 2012 NSW Premier's Literature Award, Patricia Wrightson Prize, and was shortlisted for the 2012 WA Premier's Literary Award and the Adelaide Festival Award for Children's Literature.

Kate lives in West Preston with her husband, two daughters and a bearded dragon.